TREE OF FREEDOM

When Stephanie Venable moved to Kentucky from Carolina in 1780, she knew her family was in for a great adventure. She carried an appleseed with her, just as her grandmother had done when she went to Charleston from her native France. Stephanie would nurture that seed in the wild Kentucky soil until it became her "tree of freedom." The tree wasn't merely a link with the past, but a symbol of the new way of life her pioneering family meant to build in the fresh green land of Kentucky.

This Newbery Honor book is a truly moving story, not only of the hardships of pioneer life but also of warm family relationships.

TREE OF FREEDOM

TREE OF FREEDOM

by Rebecca Caudill

ILLUSTRATED BY

Dorothy Bayley Morse

PUFFIN BOOKS

PUFFIN BOOKS
Published by the Penguin Group
Viking Penguin Inc., 40 West 23rd Street, New York, New York 10010, U.S.A.
Penguin Books Ltd, 27 Wrights Lane, London W8 5TZ, England
Penguin Books Australia Ltd, Ringwood, Victoria, Australia
Penguin Books Canada Ltd, 2801 John Street, Markham, Ontario, Canada L3R 1B4
Penguin Books (N.Z.) Ltd, 182-190 Wairau Road, Auckland 10, New Zealand

Penguin Books Ltd, Registered Offices: Harmondsworth, Middlesex, England

First published in the United States of America by Viking Penguin Inc., 1949
Published in Puffin Books 1988
1 3 5 7 9 10 8 6 4 2

Library of Congress catalog number: 88–42963
ISBN 0–14–032908–0

Printed in the United States of America
by R.R. Donnelley & Sons Company, Harrisonburg, Virginia

To James

Contents

TREE OF FREEDOM

1. One Solitary Thing

STEPHANIE VENABLE knew as soon as she opened her eyes, although she could make out nothing in the dark, that the long-awaited day had come. She was not sure if her pappy had called her name to wake her. "Steffy!" Jonathan Venable usually said when he called her early of a morning. "Time to send sleep a-packin'!" This April morning in the year 1780, however, Stephanie had heard nothing of the kind.

For a moment she lay in bed tracing the sounds she

heard: the heavy whish–sh–sh–sh– of the wind, like the restless roar of the sea, in the North Carolina piny woods along the road; the long, deep breathing of her three-year-old sister Cassie lying asleep beside her; the creaking of the bed in the opposite corner of the room as her mammy sat on the edge of it to pull on her heavy woolen stockings; the stumbling of her pappy's bare feet across the dog trot to the other room of the log house where her three brothers slept.

Nothing about those noises, she told herself, to make a body break out with goose bumps. She heard them every morning when light began to work at the window-panes and the roosters in the sweet gum tree back of the house began to flap their wings and crow. Set to this mortal sweet hour, however, when never a bird twittered sleepily in the tree crowns, nor one trickle of light leavened the darkness of the room, they spelled out a message to make a body's brain go reeling in his head.

"Noel! Rob!" Stephanie heard her pappy calling.

Always it was ten-year-old Rob who answered first. Stephanie heard him answer then. He groaned like a person with a misery, trying to prize himself out of sleep.

"Rob, are you awake?"

"Um-hum."

"Noel?"

"Yes, Pappy. It's dark as pitch."

"We're settin' out for Kentucky this mornin'. Get up an' do the feedin'. Rob?"

Stephanie heard Rob's feet on the puncheon floor as the news brought him bounding out of bed. Noel took his time about getting up. Noel took his time about everything these days, it seemed to Stephanie, as if everything he did rubbed him against the grain.

"Mind you don't wake Willie jist yet," Jonathan warned in a half-whisper, as he started back across the dog trot. "Your mammy says let him nap a mite longer."

"Steffy!"

"Yes, Mammy."

"Jump up. We're goin' today."

Bertha Venable's voice was calm in the dark—calm and steady as day a-breaking.

"Steffy, time to send sleep a-packin'."

"Yes, Pappy."

Jonathan crossed the dark room toward the big fireplace in the end of the house. Stephanie heard him jabbing the poker among the gray ashes in search of live embers with which to kindle a fire.

She slid from under the patchwork quilt quietly so as not to awaken Cassie, slipped her butternut-yellow linsey dress over her head, and buttoned herself into it. The next minute, she seated herself on the hearth beside Jonathan, drew on her long stockings, and tied her moccasins about her ankles.

Jonathan was on his hands and knees, blowing on the

embers on which he had laid pine splinters fat with pitch. A blaze leaped to life and threw gangling shadows across the floor of the room.

"I'll help you, Pappy," Stephanie announced, getting to her feet, and tossing her two buckeye-brown braids over her shoulders.

Jonathan glanced at her small, plain, pointed face, a softness in his eyes like thaw. Her eyes with the firelight on them put him in mind of the wild blue chicory that bloomed along the roadside in the fall. Of his five young uns, this was his favorite—this slim, nimble-fingered girl of thirteen who, he claimed, had every other young un in the Back Country skun a mile. Give Stephanie a job to do, he often said to Bertha, any kind of job, from grubbing sassafras sprouts out of the tobacco patch to minding a baby, and when she finished, she had fancy work to show for it.

"Get your piggin, then, an' do the milkin', while Rob an' Noel feed," Jonathan told her. "I'll be gettin' things together in one place while your mammy cooks a bite of breakfast. Reckon you won't need much fire this mornin', Berthy," he added. "After breakfast, hit can die for good."

Stephanie slipped out of the door into the cool morning. The air was scented with Bertha's early-blooming lilacs, and from Bertha's apple tree came a whiff of perfume sweet with springtime memories of the log house and the clean-swept doorway, the piny woods and the fields of broad-leaved tobacco the Venables were about to leave forever. In the dog trot she stood a moment, the cool, misty April darkness all about her, breathing in the heavy perfume. Then, firmly she felt for the piggin turned upside down on a bench in the dog trot, and started toward the stable.

"When're we leavin', Pappy?" she asked, as Jonathan joined her. Rob, followed by Noel, stumbled after them. "Sun up?"

They were halfway to the stable before Jonathan answered her. Though he walked along the well-worn path directly behind her, he was away off yonder in his mind, she knew, thinking about Kentucky, maybe, maybe stewing about Noel. All winter Jonathan had stewed about Noel. Stephanie wondered why he couldn't see things as Noel saw them. They were as plain to her as the star over the stable.

"Mebbe," said Jonathan, absent-mindedly. "Mebbe not. Jist depends."

For the next half hour the dark stable was a hive of busyness. Milking with both hands, Stephanie see-sawed long darts of milk against the bottom of the piggin and poured foam into a little trough for Willie's kitten that purred about her ankles. Jonathan brought nubbins for the cow, threw down fodder from the loft for the horse and hackled his tangled mane. Noel carried corn to the four pigs stretched full length in their wallow back of the crib, while Rob herded the three Venable sheep into the stable and fed them.

Daylight was seeping in from the east as the four of them, their stable chores finished, hurried toward the house to their breakfast of side meat fried in the skillet over live coals, and hoecake, cold milk and butter, and sweet wild honey from a honey gum tree. Breakfast on this morning, however, was to the Venable young uns a bother that had to be got out of the way before they could set out down the road for Kentucky.

"Ever' swaller of meat you don't eat'll raise up its head to ha'nt you, if ever your vittles give out," warned Jonathan. "Hit's been many a man stumbled into Harrod's Fort with ever' rib he owned a-stickin' out to be counted. An' sometimes," he added, "he didn't come from as fur a piece as Caroliny, either."

"That's fair warnin', young uns," added Bertha. "Can't anybody go far on an empty stomach."

The Venable young uns lent dull ears to such warnings, however. They weren't hungry, they said. Vittles stuck in their craws.

"Jist wrop ever'thing up, Berthy, an' bring hit along—meat, hoecake, an' all," said Jonathan. Begging young uns to do what they had no mind to do threw him into a fidget. "We won't be half a mile down the road 'fore they'll all be snivelin' for a snack. Noel," he added, "you round up the critters—the cow an' the sheep an' the pigs.

Rob, you bring the horse so's we can load the creels on him. Berthy, I don't favor tryin' to take them chickens less'n you're dead sot on givin' some Kentucky fox three square meals, but you run an' catch two hens an' a rooster, Steffy, you an' Willie, an' tie their legs good an' tight till we're ready to load 'em. Stir yourselves, now. Ain't no time to waste."

"Mammy, can I take my kitten?" asked Willie.

"Naw. No kittens," said Jonathan.

"Can I take my butterflies?" asked Rob.

"Naw. No butterflies," said Jonathan. He kicked the front log and sent a bright shower of sparks up the wide chimney. "Your butterfly-catchin' days are over, Rob," he said, looking down into the boy's brown eyes which smarted from the sting. Then he spat in the fire as if he'd been chewing something bitter he was glad to get out of his system. "Yours an' your Uncle Lucien's," he said.

Stephanie, watching Rob, saw a lonesome look settle on his face. She didn't see why he couldn't take his butterflies. Great Uncle Lucien de Monchard had taught him where to look for them on nettles and milkweeds, on huckleberry bushes and wild clover, on willow trees and pawpaw trees, and on the grayish, strong-scented stalk of the everlasting which Uncle Lucien called *immortelle*. Rob had twenty butterflies now, all different, and one great moth. The silken lined slabs of bark to which they were pinned with sharp thorns of the honey locust tree stood on a shelf over Rob's side of the bed, and color from their brittle, outstretched wings—sulphurous yellow and dark ginger and smoldering purple, the red of ripe persimmons and the sultry red of a burning sun—drenched the corner of the dimly lit room.

"Jonathan," said Bertha quietly, "ever' young un can take one thing that's his'n. Looks like as many tobacco plants as you've set out, you'd know a transplanted thing grows best if a little dirt's left cuddled up to the roots."

"Well, mebbe," agreed Jonathan, grudgingly. "But hit'll have to be sech a little mite of a thing, a body'll might' nigh have to have a spyglass to see hit. No kittens. An' no butterflies."

"But somethin'," repeated Bertha. "One solitary thing."

"Don't you mind too much about the butterflies," Stephanie said to Rob outside the door. "I 'spect there are hundreds more butterflies in Kentucky than here in North Caroliny."

"But Uncle Lucien won't be there to help me find 'em," Rob said. "And mount 'em."

"You don't need Uncle Lucien to help you," Stephanie told him. "He showed you how once. You can do it by yourself now."

"I could do it better with Uncle Lucien," said Rob.

"I know," said Stephanie. "But a body mustn't waste time frettin' over what he can't have. Some time or other, a body has to learn he can stand up to his own lick log on his own feet, and now's your time to learn it. You'd better skedaddle for the horse before Pappy sets in hollerin' for you."

The sky was a wash of pale gray light when finally two creels, crammed with trammels and pothooks, wool cards and flax hackles, griddles and spiders and skillets, sheep shears, plow irons, hoes and log chains, all of them cushioned with old blankets, were laid across the horse's back. Jonathan stood in the doorway, surveying the cabin for any small object they ought not to leave behind.

"Young uns," said Bertha, "run fetch whatever 'tis you're takin' for yourselves. We'll be leavin' in a minute."

Quicker than a body could reel off

> "Wire brier, limberlock,
> Three geese in a flock,"

Cassie darted to the chimney corner and came back hugging a wooden doll that Noel had made for her of a stick of ash. A sharp little nose and eyes and a mouth he had carved, and little bitty ears that were the spit and image of a human being's ears. In place of feet, however, he had whittled the stick broad and flat and smooth at the bottom so that Bertha, by turning the dress of red linsey back over the doll's head, could mash potatoes with it.

"This family could do with a little horse sense," Jonathan declared, when he saw that Bertha favored taking the doll. "Why saddle us with a lot of wood when that's what the whole endurin' wilderness is made out of?"

At that, Cassie let out crying and clutched the doll tightly in her arms.

"You carry it and you can take it, Cassie," soothed Bertha.

Willie, seeing Cassie's easy victory, grew bold. "Mammy," he begged, "couldn't I take my kitten? I'd carry it."

"Naw. No kittens," declared Jonathan. "I told you so once."

"You can get another pet in Kentucky, Willie," soothed Bertha. "A coon, maybe. Coons make likely pets."

"I know what I'm takin'," said Willie, darting up the ladder to the loft. In a minute he came down the ladder backwards, carrying in his hand a ball-shaped puzzle Uncle Lucien had carved of the gall of a scrub pine tree. Many a winter evening Noel and Stephanie, sprawled on the floor, had worked by firelight, taking the puzzle apart and putting it together again. Separated into twelve oddly shaped little pieces, it seemed a thing a body couldn't possibly get into a ball again, not if he worked at it till Christmas. Then, all of a sudden, one little bitty piece would slip into another. Then another piece would settle into its place, and another, and, finally, there would be the ball, no bigger than a body's thumb.

"Stuff it in your shirt, Willie," said Bertha, before

Jonathan could say, "Naw. No puzzles. Nothin' at all made by your Uncle Lucien."

"Rob, what are you takin'?" asked Bertha.

"I reckon I'll just find me somethin' when we settle down in the wilderness, Mammy," said Rob, glancing at Stephanie.

"Steffy?"

Stephanie hesitated. All through the winter she had had her heart set on an old French looking glass that had come to the New World with the de Monchards, and had been handed down from Grandmammy Linney to Bertha, to be given to Stephanie some day when she should have a cabin of her own. It was an oblong object, a foot wide, framed with walnut carved all around with fragile curlicues, and topped with a golden bouquet in a vase of gold. To leave it behind wrought an emptiness the like of which the loss of Rob's butterflies was as nothing. Every which way a body might turn in the Kentucky wilderness, he was apt to see mottled gauzy wings—yellow and black, pale spring-green and ginger—fanning the air, but let a body look till blindness overtook him, and he'd never find Grandmammy's French looking glass.

"If you're a-thinkin' of that lookin' glass, Steffy," said Jonathan, reading her thoughts, "naw. Scotch that notion right away. Nobody packs a lookin' glass across the mountains."

Stephanie swallowed hard. No, she knew nobody in

his right mind packed a fancy French looking glass across the mountains. It couldn't be eaten and it couldn't be worn. It couldn't mold a bullet, chop down a tree, nor fend off an Indian.

Worst of all, in Jonathan's sight, the looking glass had de Monchard connections. Poor Jonathan! The de Monchards, according to him, had heaped a sight of disgrace on him one way or another. They were always sitting and thinking, he complained. Or fiddling. Or piddling. Or reading out of a book. Or brewing notions as acrid as black cohosh tea. And how they could fritter away time! To think of a grown man whittling for hours on the gall of a scrub pine, or traipsing after butterflies the way Uncle Lucien had, when the piny woods were full of deer and the Waxhaw was overflowing with speckled trout. The de Monchards were plumb beyond a man's understanding, Jonathan said.

It seemed queer to Stephanie that her pappy had married Marguerite de Monchard Linney's daughter, Bertha, and that in spite of himself he was as no account without her as a powder horn without powder. He himself said so when he was feeling good.

"Sam Coldiron's a-comin' over in his oxcart purty soon to pick up the things we can't take," announced Jonathan. "I've already settled with him on that lookin' glass. He's paid me a Spanish milled dollar for hit. One Spanish milled dollar in Kentucky's wuth a wagon load of that Continental stuff they're coinin' comin' an' goin' at Philadelphy."

Stephanie glanced at the looking glass, for a moment her shoulders wilted like a tobacco plant wanting rain.

"I'll have to think a minute what I'm takin', Mammy," she said.

"Noel," Bertha asked, "what are you takin'?"

"Nothin'," Noel answered, a sullen, hurt look in his lean, freckled face, a smoldering fire in his eyes that were as gray as steel, and as hard to bore through. "Nothin' 'cept some notions in my head," he said. "And," he added, looking straight at Jonathan, "my dulcimore on my back."

"Noel!" Jonathan stormed, as red as a red bird with rage. "That dulcimore's a-stayin' on this here side of the mountains."

"Why?" asked Noel, never taking his eyes off his pappy.

"Why? 'Cause you'd sure be a purty sight a-showin' up at Harrod's Fort with that plague-take-hit thing!" sputtered Jonathan. "An' besides," he added, "your rifle's load enough. What do you think your back's made out of? Iron?"

"It's his back, ain't it, Jonathan?" put in Bertha.

"Can't the boy never grow up, Berthy?" hollered Jonathan like a clap of thunder, as he turned on his wife. "You jist humor him in his Tidewater notions. Noel," he turned back to the boy, "we ain't movin' a step from this place till you say good-by to that dulcimore. An' all the foolish notions you brung from your Uncle Lucien's along with hit."

"If Noel promises not to play the dulcimore in your hearin', Jonathan," Bertha said, her voice cooling as a wind blowing off the sea, "and promises not to pluck a solitary string, let him have it. 'Twon't hurt him any. An' a little music won't hurt Kentucky, either."

She eased over to Jonathan and laid her hand on his arm as gently as she would have touched Cassie.

"Let's let the boy have one thing he wants, Jonathan," she begged. "You try seein' things his way once, an' he'll begin seein' things your way. He's got his rifle, ain't he, as well as his dulcimore? He'll use it like a man. See if he don't. That's enough to ask of a boy, ain't it—that he use a rifle like a man?"

A full minute passed before Jonathan made a move. Then he turned and stumbled across the dog trot toward the gate, muttering as he did so that if he had ever had any notion of a dulcimer bringing up the rear of the Venable train, he'd have stayed in the Caroliny Back Country the rest of his borned days and let the tax collector plague him right down to the burying ground.

"Steffy," he said grumblingly, "if you're a-takin' anything, bring hit a-runnin', whatever 'tis."

In that single moment Stephanie knew what she was taking.

In the smokehouse she broke the cobwebs that sealed a warped old calabash. Reaching her fingers inside, she took one solitary apple seed of the many Bertha had saved, and dropped it into the deerskin pouch that hung about her waist, tracing in her mind as she did so the long, strange journey of the apples through which the seed had come. Bertha's Back Country tree had grown from seed she had saved from an apple that grew on Grandmammy Linney's tree in Charleston. And Grandmammy Linney, when she was thirteen-year-old Marguerite de Monchard, had brought her seed from an apple that grew on a tree in the yard of her old home in France. The Trees of St. Jean de Maurienne, they were called, for the little French village from which Grandmammy came.

Stephanie, hurrying back to the house, decided to keep her reasons for planting the seed a secret from every living soul but Noel. He would understand them, she knew, because they were akin to the notions he was carrying in his head as he set out for the wilderness of Kentucky.

2. Journey's End

"NOEL," said Jonathan as the Venables assembled at the gate, "you bring up the rear an' drive the cow an' the pigs. Rob, the sheep are yourn to mammy. Steffy, you carry the kettle of salt. Mind you keep this here patch of deerskin tied over it tight. Here, Willie, you an' Cassie, let me h'ist you into the creels."

From that moment, day after day, from the first faint

orange that blurred the east to owl light, the Venables were on the move, pushing westward toward the sunset in whose rays, somewhere, stood Harrod's Fort. It seemed to Stephanie, when the mute, purplish peaks of the Appalachians frowned down upon them from terrible far heights and the narrow mountain passes shrouded them in green gloom, that it was a bold thing to have pitted the puny strength of the Venables against the lumbering mountain ranges.

It was like the shepherd boy David going out to fight the Philistine giant, the story of which Bertha had often read to the Venable young uns from an old Huguenot Bible, in strange words which they understood but which they never spoke. The Bible was packed away carefully in one of the creels, but Stephanie needed no book to conjure up for her the mighty mail-clad Goliath defying singlehanded the armies of Israel, and the young un David defying Goliath.

Pourquoi sortiriez-vous pour vous ranger en bataille? Ne suis-je point Philistin, et vous, n'êtes pas serviteurs de Saül? Choisissez l'un d'entre vous, et qu'il descende vers moi.

On they went, on and on, and on, trudging along the hatchet-blazed trails where others unknown to them had gone before and left a heartening sign for them to follow; moving spiritedly on the clean-cut buffalo traces; threading narrow mountain defiles; crossing swollen streams on clumsy rafts built by Jonathan and Noel of saplings tied together with grapevines; hiding in dense canebrakes at the sign of red men; and sleeping at night in the protection of steep rocks or fallen tree butts with their feet to the fire to bake the cold and damp out of their bodies.

When the journey was new, Stephanie's feet had carried her over the rough, steep trail like a silken seed spun in the wind. After a month of climbing, however, her feet felt as heavy as the salt-filled iron kettle. Her yellow dress, trim in the waist and full of skirt, which she had worn day and night on the journey, was bedraggled with rain and dew, with sleeping on pine boughs and stumbling over rocks, with stretching flat on her stomach to drink from mountain springs, and with scrambling up steep slopes in search of the fiery leaves of wintergreen with which to stay her gnawing hunger, now that Bertha, in an effort to stretch their dwindling supply of meal, doled out ever smaller wedges of hoecake at mealtime.

"I'm so full of scratches I reckon I'll have to be sewed up all over when we get to Kentucky," she complained to Jonathan one May evening when the tallest of the mountain peaks loomed darkly behind them and they made their way through chinquapin thickets and hazel patches growing tightly in the open places of the foothills.

There was no sign from Jonathan that he heard her.

"Didn't you tell us before we left home, Pappy," she

asked, "that when we passed that beech tree with 'Peter Brumbach, 1777' carved on it, we'd be might' nigh in hollerin' distance of Harrod's Fort?"

"Did I?" Jonathan asked.

"Yes. Don't you recollect you did?"

Jonathan did not answer. Skirting a hill, he began hurrying as Stephanie did not remember he had hurried since they left the Back Country, glancing now and then over his shoulder to see that the Venables behind him were keeping the file closed.

Stephanie hurried, too. They crossed a shallow creek, picked their way among thickets of alder and ozier and a grove of sycamores, and climbed the high slope of a hill. Halfway to the top, in an open place grown over with coarse buffalo grass and dewberry vines, Jonathan stopped, lifted his rifle from his shoulders, and let it slide through his fingers till the butt of it rested on the ground. Stephanie, glad of a chance to rest, set down her kettle of salt, and slumped on the grass at his feet.

"We'll wait till they overtake us," Jonathan told her.

Stephanie watched the rest of the Venables crossing the creek at the foot of the hill, her mother first, walking with a stout hickory stick. Bertha's gray bonnet tied under her chin had fallen between her shoulders, and left her hair for the sun to shine on—hair that had once been rich buckeye-brown like Stephanie's, and soft about her face, but was now the dull color of the grayish cottonade dress she wore.

Stephanie noticed how steadily her mammy moved along the uncertain trail. All the long, hard way from the Back Country she had marched along evenly, seldom hurrying, seldom slackening her pace, the slow sing-song pattern of her footsteps like the regular beat of the long ballads Noel had sung to Stephanie to the twanging of the dulcimer in the Back Country hayloft.

> "Lady Ouncebell was buried in the high chancel,
> Lord Lovill in the choir;
> Lady Ouncebell's breast sprung out a sweet rose,
> Lord Lovill's a bunch of sweet brier."

Behind Bertha came the horse. He had grown up with a regal name, Rex, having been born when kings were less hated and Americans less headstrong; but by reason of the patience with which he carried the load heaped on his back, and the promise that in the Kentucky wilderness his lifelong lot would be cursed with breaking stump-filled new ground, and dragging logs, with carrying heavy loads, and being ridden to and fro, he had been rechristened Job by the Venable young uns. Jonathan had led him the first part of the journey. Now the horse followed in the train, without halter or bridle, his feet slow and steady, his eyes big and watery and patient.

Besides the heavy creels, Job carried a pack saddle strapped on his back, and a little cage of hickory twigs in which rode the rooster and the two hens Bertha was taking into the wilderness. In the creels rode Cassie and Willie, one on either side, sitting on the bedding with which Bertha had covered the tools and utensils. At that moment, both of them were dozing in the May sunshine, the tops of the creels laced securely about them so that only their heads showed.

Behind the horse came Rob. In the month of travel, however, Rob had come to mean to the Venables something more than a ten-year-old boy, for so closely was he companioned with the sheep he was mammying that Noel once accused him of bleating in answer to his name. But Bertha, noting how Rob by day watched out for grassy mounds where the sheep might fill their stomachs, and by night bedded them together and curled up against them to sleep, declared that there had never been a better shepherd boy, not even King David himself, and that when they reached Kentucky and she could get at her cards, and Noel and Jonathan could make her a spinning wheel and a loom, he should have the first shirt from the wool on the sheep's backs.

At the end of the train marched Noel, driving the four troublesome pigs and Brownie the cow. Noel's rifle that he carried on his shoulder was every whit as long as he. On his back was strapped the dulcimer, now as silent a thing as a human being bereft of his tongue.

On the long journey Noel had made himself handy, and never once had he crossed Jonathan or riled him. But his steely, hurt eyes seemed to say to Jonathan,

"You can lash me with your tongue and whip me with a hickory stick till the mountains fall into the sea, but you can't make me leave behind one single jot nor tittle that I learned from Uncle Lucien. Not one."

The troubled look Noel wore was, to Stephanie, the one real hardship on the long journey. Morning, noon, and night, it was heavy on her like a load she couldn't lay down. Not even when she whispered to Noel about the seed of the apple tree one evening did he thaw out completely, but she could see he was warmed by the knowledge.

Watching Noel cross the creek with the sun shining on his thatch of sun-bleached hair, Stephanie recalled the Back Country wrangling between her brother and her pappy—a wrangling that was as prickly as a thorn bush, and as hard to grub out. She remembered the day, late in the fall just passed, when Jonathan came home from a summer sojourn in the Kentucky wilderness, bringing with him a treasury warrant signed by Governor Thomas Jefferson's Kentucky land commissioners, guaranteeing him four hundred acres of Kentucky land on which he had planted a corn patch the year before. Come spring, announced Jonathan, as jubilant as a spring robin, as soon as the weather broke and a body could get through the mountain passes, the Venables would strike out for Kentucky before the tax collector could make his rounds and start snooping in the Venable smokehouse and down the Venable potato hole.

Sitting there on the Kentucky hillside, Stephanie recollected every word her pappy and mammy said that fall day back in their log house on the banks of the Waxhaw.

"If we're goin' in the spring, Jonathan," Bertha said, "then now's a good time to let Noel go to see Uncle Lucien in Charleston."

"What would Noel be doin' that for?" Jonathan asked.

"You don't need him here," Bertha said. "The winter's work won't be the same as if we'd be stayin' forever in the Back Country. We won't be takin' a whole passel of things into the wilderness, so there'll be nothin' in the way of goose yokes and hoe handles and scythe handles for you an' Noel to whittle at. Noel might as well be learnin' the useful things Uncle Lucien can teach him. Readin' for one thing."

"Berthy," declared Jonathan, "you're a-goin' to ruin that young un. Wantin' Uncle Lucien to teach him to read! Look at me! I can't read. But show me a man, point out to me jist one man who can bark a squirrel as clean, or chop down a tree as fast, or stave off starvation any better than I can. That's all Noel or anybody else needs to know in the wilderness. Besides," he added, "there won't be nothin' to read in Kentucky."

"We don't aim to let Kentucky stay a wilderness, do we?" Bertha argued. "Readin' might come in handy some day. And now's Noel's last chance to learn."

"You're jist a-ruinin' that boy, Berthy, I'm a-tellin'

you," Jonathan warned. "Puttin' high an' mighty notions in his head. An' your Uncle Lucien'll jist add the crownin' touches."

It took a week of rain to win Jonathan to Bertha's way of thinking, Stephanie recollected. After seven days of downpour with seven Venables shut up in the house and nothing of importance to occupy the menfolks, Jonathan said if Uncle Lucien could teach Noel anything at all, it would be better than having the boy mope around in the chimney corner all winter.

Noel came home in March, carrying strapped on his back a little instrument with a short neck, three wire strings, and four heart-shaped holes carved two above and two below its slim waist. He had made it with Uncle Lucien's help.

"What's that thing?" inquired Jonathan.

"A dulcimore," Noel told him.

"What's hit for?" Jonathan demanded.

"To make music," Noel said.

"To think that a boy of mine'd be packin' that thing around 'stid of a rifle!" Jonathan raged. "Hit's a crownin' disgrace! I don't want to hear a solitary string plucked in this house, Noel. Nary a one. D'you hear?"

Noel didn't pluck the strings in the house. But out in the stable loft where he hid the dulcimer, he sat on the hay with the instrument across his lap, and as he twanged the strings with a stubby piece of leather, he sang to Stephanie all the songs he had learned from

Uncle Lucien. Stephanie, her red lips parted, her blue eyes opened wide, sat entranced with the strange, sweet strumming. It was a low and lonesome sound, like the moaning wind in the piny woods, to match the words Noel sang.

"There was a little ship and she sailed upon the sea,
And she went by the name of the Golden Willow Tree;
As she sailed upon the lone and the lonesome low,
As she sailed upon the lonesome sea."

Even when the words were livelier, as they often were, the strumming was sad as a funeral.

"I swapped me a horse and got me a mare,
And then I rode from fair to fair.
Tum a wing waw waddle,
Tum a jack straw straddle,
Tum a John paw faddle,
Tum a long way home.

"I swapped my mare and got me a cow,
And in that trade I just learned how.
Tum a wing waw waddle. . . ."

Sometimes Noel held the dulcimer across his knees without plucking the strings while he told Stephanie all that he had done and seen and heard at Uncle Lucien's.

Charleston was the hub in the war for freedom in the South, Noel told her, and Uncle Lucien's house in Charleston was the meeting place of South Carolina patriots who sneaked in at night, right under the noses of the British, and made their plans. They vowed to fight for their freedom, old Uncle Lucien the loudest of all, as long as one of them had breath in his body. If the British took Georgia, the patriots dared them to lay hands on Charleston, Noel said. If they should take Charleston, the patriots would make for the backlands, join Francis Marion, hide out in the swamps, and plague the life out of the British.

It was more than freedom the patriots were fighting for, Noel said, as Stephanie listened eagerly. If once the patriots could wrest their freedom from the British king, they could form a government of their own, in which there would be no kings but only men, and all men would have equal rights, and every man would have the duty of the government resting on his own shoulders. Such a government, Uncle Lucien had told Noel, was an old, old dream of many wise men, but not yet had men been able to throw off the yokes that confined them, or break the chains that bound them so that the chance to form a government of free men might be theirs.

Now, in America, Uncle Lucien had said, men—plain, honest men, buckskinned men and Tidewater merchants, Massachusetts farmers and Philadelphia lawyers and Virginia planters, shoemakers and coopers, surveyors and builders of river flatboats, and keepers of ordinaries—were about to wrest from a king that chance.

If the chance was theirs, they could make a pattern of free men for all the world to live by.

If the chance was theirs! Uncle Lucien, Noel said, harped on that till a body could mighty nigh feel his ankles straining against chains that were bound to give way, so mighty was the force against them. Let the patriots hold together a while longer, Uncle Lucien urged the little band hiding in his Charleston cellar. One winter longer. One summer longer—a summer ghastly, as summers always were, with fever and ague and smallpox. Their chance would come—if they held together just a little longer.

If only he had a rifle, Noel had told Stephanie, making her giddy with his courage, he'd go back and fight alongside the patriots.

It was a rainy April night, Stephanie recollected, that Jonathan glanced up to the big buck antlers above the fireplace and saw his rifle was gone. He caught Noel before the boy had gone far, and whipped him soundly.

"This here rifle's aimin' to go to Kentucky, Noel," Jonathan said as he laid it back in the arms of the antlers. "Hit's got a job to do, feedin' us an' clearin' the land of varmints an' makin' Kentucky fit for livin'. See you leave hit whar 'tis. An'," he added, "see you stay with hit. You're needed in Kentucky a whole sight worse than them red-hot patriots in Charleston need you, or George Washington, or that bunch of scoundrels in that

Continental Congress in Philadelphy that think o' nothin' but taxes. D'you hear?"

Noel had answered nary a word.

"D'you hear, Noel?" Jonathan shouted. "Answer me."

"Yes," said Noel, and wrath boiled up in his gray eyes like thick, dark molasses boiling up in a vat.

"Yes, what?"

"Yes, Pappy."

"Can't figger out what's a-goin' on in your head," went on Jonathan. "Except I mought 'a' known your Uncle Lucien'd plant some foolishness there, jist like I told your mammy he would. Here's our chance to move clean away an' leave all this arguin' an' wranglin' an' fightin' an' taxin' behind, an' get rich to boot on land that's as black as your mammy's skillet. Tell me, Noel, what's wrong with that?"

"Nothin', Pappy," answered Noel, "from where you're standin'." Then he had drawn up inside his shell like a terrapin that somebody has stepped on, and he had never come out, not even when Jonathan traded the last of his tobacco crop for the second-hand rifle Noel carried on his shoulder. Stephanie wondered if he ever would come out.

As soon as Noel crossed the creek, Jonathan shouldered his rifle and cut out across the hill which sloped gently to the crest, then leveled off like a giant tree-grown table top. Great bushy crowns of oak and popple, chestnut and beech, laced together with grapevines, fashioned a green roof overhead. Stephanie, stretching her legs to keep up with her pappy, and looking out for briers and brambly bushes in the undergrowth, noticed slim fingers of gold reaching in from the west among the black butts of the trees.

"Hurry, Steffy!" Jonathan called.

She shifted the kettle to her other hand, and hurried to catch up with him.

"Look over yonder towards the sun," Jonathan told her.

Stephanie found herself standing on the sheer edge of the tableland, with the earth dropping in a plumb line hundreds of feet below. Setting down her kettle, she shaded her eyes with her hand and gazed thirstily at the wide horizon, trying to harvest all at once the wonder of the world that lay spread out below her—a vast world, with lush green meadows and wooded hollows rippling away as far as she could see. All her life she had been heading into mountains. Now the mountains were behind her, out of her life, and the world was wide and ongoing, its springtime green rimmed far off with a gauzy haze the color of frost-blue plums.

"Well, what d'you see, Steffy?" prodded Jonathan.

"Kentucky, Pappy," she said. "But why didn't you tell us it looked all—all wide like this, and green, and full of sky?" she demanded, half scoldingly. "For two whole years you've talked about Kentucky, but nary a thing have you mentioned but black land and wild critters and varmints."

"I didn't have the words, I reckon, Steffy," Jonathan said. "I knowed all along I wasn't makin' you young uns see Kentucky the fine way hit is."

While the others threaded their way across the wooded table top, Stephanie continued to stare at the new land they were at last about to enter and to claim.

"I reckon nobody could have told us Kentucky was like this, Pappy," she said at last. "Nobody, that is, without book learnin', like Noel."

"Does book learnin' do that for a body?" he asked.

"Of course, Pappy!" Stephanie assured him. "Didn't you ever want to learn to read?" she asked. "Not in your whole life? Didn't you have any Uncle Lucien to teach you things out of a book?"

"So far as I been able to jedge, readin's jist a sort of fancy work," Jonathan said. "Whar's hit ever got your Uncle Lucien? Nowhars. Whar'll hit ever get Noel? Nowhars, either. Hit don't have ever'day value like knowin' how to hit a high-tailin' deer, or how to boil down salt, or what to do when a b'ar disputes the right of way, or how to find yourself when you're lost as a lunatic in the woods. That's the onliest kind of learnin' we got use for in Kentucky right now."

Stephanie glanced up at him. He was a big man, and now that the green meadow of Kentucky lay before him and the long stretch of the Appalachian Mountains walled him off from the North Carolina tax collector, he stood as tall and as proud as any king. In the bosom of his worn old red linsey shirt was the warrant for his Kentucky land, and from his belt and across his shoulders were slung the weapons and the implements that made him master of the wilderness—his bullet bag, his ax, his hunting knife in a leather sheath, his powder horn protected by a patch of deerskin, and his long rifle. His old coonskin cap which he wore when he left the Back Country was now folded underneath his belt, and as he stood bareheaded in the sun, he put Stephanie in mind of the stern, Abraham-like mountains through which they had come, his graying hair and his weathered face with its sharp nose jutting above his odd assortment of garments and weapons like lichen-covered rock above the tree line.

"How old were you, Pappy, when you ran away from home?" Stephanie asked.

"Ten," he said.

"Just the age of Rob," Stephanie mused. "What made you run away?"

"My pappy and mammy died," he said. "I didn't like the folks that took me in. They lived in Maryland. I sneaked out one night when hit was rainin' an' started runnin', an' I never stopped till I got to North Caroliny. I been on my own ever since."

For a minute he stood looking out over the valley.

"I'll never forget my first job," he added, "diggin'

'taters for your Grandpappy Linney. He was a Quaker, an' he lived in a Quaker settlement on the banks of the Tar. I recollect how your mammy looked the first time I set eyes on her, too. She wasn't any bigger'n a minute, an' she was the spit an' image of you. Eyes exactly the color of yourn."

Color tinged Jonathan's leathery face, as if he were plagued at having said so much.

"Why are you askin' sech questions?" he wanted to know.

"Just because," smiled Stephanie. She looked at him closely, thinking how well he knew the way to tame the wild country that lay before them. Such knowledge wasn't printed in books, she told herself. It wasn't knowledge the Linneys possessed, or the de Monchards. But a body had to have it, and no mistake, if he meant to come to terms with the wilderness.

"The woods were your Uncle Lucien, weren't they, Pappy?" she asked.

"Humph!" snorted Jonathan. "Whatever put that fancy question in your head?"

"Oh, nothin' much," she said, smiling up at him.

Bertha came in sight through the trees.

"Hurry up, ever'body!" shouted Jonathan. "Noel, hurry!"

At last they stood together on the ledge, Job and Brownie alongside them, the sheep foraging and the pigs rooting around them.

"Out yonder," Jonathan announced, proud as a peacock strutting its showy tail fanwise. "Off in that direction," he said, pointing northwest. "Little bit further than you can see, mebbe. 'Bout as far as that last line of blue hills that look like a blue cloud restin' flat on the ground. Right in there'll be Harrod's Fort."

The Venables stared greedily, shading their eyes from the late sun in an effort to pierce the far, faint blue line.

"I see it!" cried Rob, pointing a finger in the direction of the hills.

"Whereabouts?" asked Noel, crowding against him.

Stephanie followed with her eyes the line Rob described, but in all the wide, green valley she could see no fort.

"Look!" cried Rob, now pointing his finger toward the west. "Look, Pappy! What's that? Buffalo?"

"Jist a laurel patch, I reckon," said Jonathan. It pleasured him mightily that he could name with certainty sights his family had never seen. "If we'd 'a' come out a little north of here, Rob," he said, "close to one of them thar big licks, you'd see buffalo. Thousands of 'em. If ever'body stirs their stumps right smart now," he added, "we ought to make Harrod's Fort in a matter of two days. Three at most."

Once more they moved forward, new life swelling up within them, causing them to forget their weariness. By a round-about way they descended the hill and cut out across the valley, marching through woods and thicket and meadow, laurel grove and hazel patch, all their senses alert, their eyes trained on the farthest line of low hills.

Toward evening, on the third day, Stephanie, traipsing at Jonathan's heels, stopped suddenly.

"Listen!" she said. "What's that, Pappy?"

"Sounds like choppin' to me," said Jonathan. "Don't hit to you? Somebody buildin' hisself a cabin, I reckon. Hit means we're a-gettin' close to the Fort."

Farther on she stopped again. "What's that?" she asked.

Jonathan laughed.

"Looks like you forgot all you ever knowed, Steffy," he teased. "Or else you don't rightly believe we're about to our journey's end. That's a man a-plowin' new ground, an' his ox ain't a bit different from a Caroliny ox. They all want a lot of geein' an' hawin' an' proddin' with a pole to keep 'em movin'."

As the sun was slipping behind the rim of the valley, the Venables came out of the woods into a clearing, and saw Harrod's Fort looming before them. Like a great log box it hulked, with three blockhouses guarding it, and all about the square a stout oaken stockade reared high in the air, the earth rammed hard against the roots of it. It shamed everything the Back Country could brag about, thought Stephanie. Not in all of

Hillsborough, where her pappy had once taken her on horse-swapping day, was there anything so eternal great big as Harrod's Fort.

Like a horse on the home stretch, Jonathan hurried across the clearing, Stephanie at his heels, still clutching the black kettle, now only half full of salt, seeing everything, hearing everything, staring in astonishment at the many men who came and went outside the high stockade, or stood about in knots, talking together.

Not even in Hillsborough, nor at the Presbyterian camp meeting had she seen so many men at one time. Most of them, she noticed, wore buckskin clothes like Jonathan's and Noel's, with tight leggings that weren't always getting caught in the briers, and roomy shirts in the loose bosom of which could be carried all sorts of things a body might need in the woods—parched corn and jerk, tow for cleaning a rifle barrel, and a pouch for money, if a body had money, and valuable papers, if a body had valuable papers, as Jonathan had.

But there were men in other clothes, too—outlandish clothes that belonged in the Tidewater, and in faraway cities to the north. There were men wearing tight breeches with buckles at the knee in which shone paste jewels, low leather shoes fastened with square buckles, long silk stockings, waistcoats of velvet, cravats tied at the throat in a large flowing bow, and low-crowned, broad-brimmed beaver hats. One man wore an officer's hat, the brim turned up sharply at front and decorated with a silk cockade of black and white. His hair was powdered with flour and tallow, and cued to a fare-you-well.

"Pappy," whispered Stephanie, "is that the governor of Virginny?"

"Governor Tom Jefferson?" laughed Jonathan. "You'd know him, Steffy, by his red hair, they say." Jonathan talked low in his throat. "Ain't none of them fellers a governor," he said. "They're speculators, most likely, that the governor has to watch. Slick, land-hungry scoundrels, a lot of 'em are, apt as not. Agents, mebbe, for big companies of rich men all along the Atlantic. The fancier a man's rigged out, the fancier a land-grabbin' scoundrel he is, way I figger hit."

A buckskinned man, spying them, hurried to meet them.

"Howdy, Strangers!" he boomed, his voice ringing with welcome.

"Howdy!" said Jonathan.

"Back Country folks, I'll be bound!" said the man. "Jist a-gettin' in, I'll be bound! Ain't you?"

"Jist a-gettin' in," replied Jonathan. "Reckon my folks can put up here in the Fort for the night?"

By that time the Venables were faced with a dozen curious onlookers.

"Fort's mighty crowded," spoke up one man. "Land-crazy families been a-comin' in here from ever' which direction for a month now. Reckon they can always scrouge one more in, though."

"Huntin' land?" asked the first man.

"Got my land," Jonathan told him.

"Got a warrant?" asked the man.

"Got a warrant," said Jonathan. "Thought mebbe I'd find the surveyor somewhars about."

"He's in that thar blockhouse, him an' the deputy," spoke up another man. "Goin' to knock off for supper soon. Have to hurry if you want to do business before dark."

Upon that advice, the Venables moved toward the heavy gates of the stockade which stood open inward, the buckskinned crowd, rimmed with men in outlandish dress, traipsing after. Close to Jonathan walked Stephanie, staring at the strange faces, sniffing the rich smell of venison broiling over an open fire in the square, hearing from within the stockade scraps of homey sounds that gathered a tired, homesick body in and made it feel at home—sounds of womenfolks talking together, of the chopping of wood for a fire, of the deep bawling of cows waiting to be milked, of the keyed-up bawling of young calves wanting their supper, of the shouts of little tykes playing whoopy hide, of mothers scolding and calling to their young uns to come and get their vittles.

Through the heavy gates they went, toward the nearest blockhouse, Stephanie trying to attend to everything at once—seeing that Job followed after them through the gates, that Rob got the sheep in, that Brownie and the pigs were not left behind, and that she was not separated from her pappy by the crowd of curious men who were bound and determined to hear what the surveyor had to say to Jonathan. Noel's dulcimer, she noticed, created no stir at all. Harrod's Fort, she decided, had seen outlandish things before.

Inside the blockhouse Stephanie found herself scrouged beside her pappy when he stood before the long puncheon table at which two men were seated. A ledger lay open on the table in front of them, and in it one of the men wrote with a gray goose quill dipped in a purplish pokeberry ink smelling of alum and vinegar.

"Howdy!" said the man nearest the door.

"Howdy!" replied Jonathan. "You the surveyor?"

"That's right," said the man. "May's my name. And Jim Douglas here," he nodded toward the man who wrote in the ledger, "he's my deputy. Got a claim?"

"Yessiree," answered Jonathan proudly, reaching inside the bosom of his shirt and bringing out the warrant, now soiled with much handling and journeying.

"Name's Jonathan Venable?" asked the surveyor opening up the warrant.

"Jonathan Venable," said Jonathan.

The surveyor squinted to see the words in the dim light of the blockhouse. He read aloud:

"Jonathan Venable this day appeared and claimed a preemption of four hundred acres of land, he being a settler in this country, who made corn in the year 1778, as appears by testimony, lying on the waters of Salt River, at a spring with the J. V. cut on each tree. The court are of the opinion that the said Venable has a right to the preemption of four hundred acres of land according to law, and that a certificate issue for same. Signed,

William Fleming, Chief Justice,
James Barbour,
Edmund Lyne,
Stephan Trigg."

"Got some other claims out Salt River way," announced the deputy, laying down his goose quill. "I'll be startin' about sunup tomorrow. Might as well survey yourn first. Reckon you're anxious to get a corn patch planted right away," he added. "Winter's been so hard through here, folks is starvin' to death."

"This all the help you got to clear your land, Venable?" the surveyor asked, smiling at Stephanie.

Jonathan looked down at her and smiled, too.

"Jist part of the help," he said. "The best part, I reckon."

3. Black Kentucky Land

THE VENABLES slept in the Fort that night, stretched out close together on the ground. All about them slept other families who, likewise, had come to raise cabins and make clearings on corn-patch or tomahawk claims. A passel of them from the Carolinas —from the Catawba, the Yadkin, and the Haw in the Back Country, and from the Neuse and Drowning Creek and the Little Pee Dee farther east—had followed the same trail the Venables followed, had scaled the same mountains, crossed the same waters, filed through the same gaps and notches. To Stephanie they were almost kinfolks.

The greater number of the families, however, had come into Kentucky from another direction. Starting from Massachusetts and New York, Pennsylvania and New Jersey, they had drifted down the Ohio from Fort Pitt to Corn Island in big, clumsy arks which they abandoned when the perilous voyage was done. Others had come from Virginia, across mountains and through gaps of their own.

Stretched out on the ground, too, slept the solitary menfolks—the speculators and the agents, the hunters and the trappers, and those who had come merely to see for themselves this wonder of Kentucky which was the talk at supper tables and around open firesides from one end of the Atlantic seaboard to the other.

Dark had scarcely settled on the Fort when Stephanie snuggled down under an old blanket beside Cassie and fought sleep for a pinch of a minute. All about her she heard the talk of menfolks and womenfolks, and though she paid little attention to the words that were said, she rested herself in the gentle sound. In a corner of the stockade cows tethered near the spring bawled, horses bit one another, and dogs barked. Lightning bugs flickered about the Fort, and in the row of cabins along one wall of the stockade, the light from sputtering candles glowed softly through the open doorways, and through the windowpanes of heavy paper slick with bear's grease.

Turning on her back, and stretching her aching legs,

Stephanie gazed for a spell into the wide sky, now sprinkled with stars that burned like signal fires over them, felt for the apple seed in the deerskin pouch still tied about her waist, and fell asleep.

At the first glimmering of morning light, Bertha Venable shook the Venable young uns from their sleep and set them at their tasks. Stephanie she sent to milk the cow, Rob to round up the sheep, and Noel to bring up Job for reloading. Cassie, too, had to get up and let Bertha fold the blanket under which she had slept. Then Bertha put Willie to minding the little tyke and keeping her out of other folks' business while she broiled slices of venison for which she had exchanged a spoonful of salt.

Piggin in hand, Stephanie went across the square looking for Brownie, stopping on the way to peep through the doorway of the schoolhouse that stood inside the Fort. It did beat all, she thought to herself, how her pappy hadn't told them half the wonders of Kentucky. Not once had he squeaked about a schoolhouse.

At the spring she found Rob separating the Venable sheep from those belonging to other families.

"Jeeminy, criminy, Steffy!" he called out when he saw her, his voice a mixture of awe and caution. "Did you ever think you'd see such an eternal big thing in the wilderness as this here Fort? Just look at them blockhouses! Couldn't an Indian get within a mile of this place, I bet!"

Stephanie turned and studied the big, stalwart blockhouses which lorded it over the square.

"Supposin' Indians did?" she said.

"Let 'em try!" bragged Rob, as bold as any Long Hunter, now that the red men were nowhere about. "Even if they caught folks in here unawares, the forters could last out the siege, I bet."

He began pointing out to her all the handy things within the stockade—a second spring near the center of the square, a hominy block, a blacksmith shop, the firing platform built along the stockade.

"Did you see the schoolhouse?" she asked.

"Yeah," he said, "but who's a-goin' to waste time a-sittin' in a schoolhouse like a bump on a log gettin' book learnin'?"

Stephanie scowled at him. "Rob," she declared, "you sure do take after Pappy."

"There's one thing they ain't got," said Rob, paying her no mind. "All these people comin' an' goin' have tamped down the ground so hard, there ain't a blade of grass inside this whole stockade for a sheep to nibble at."

Stephanie laughed. "I 'spect as long as you live, you'll see things through a sheep's eyes, Rob. Have you seen Brownie?"

"Right over there she is by the stockade," said Rob. "She's down, and she looks like she don't ever mean to get up."

"Maybe you'd better help me get her up, so I can milk her," Stephanie told him. "Wonder what Mammy's big hurry is?"

"She don't like fortin'," said Rob.

"How do you know?"

"I heard her whisperin' to Pappy last night. Says she never smelled such a smell in her life as there is in this Fort, what with all sorts of human bein's, and all manner of dumb critters bein' shut up in the stockade ever' night, and flies buzzin' about a body's vittles and musquiters fiddlin' in a body's ears."

"Why, Rob!" confessed Stephanie, recollecting the welcome smell of wood smoke and broiling meat that had greeted them the evening before. "It smelled plumb good to me."

"Stick your nose down close to that spring once," commanded Rob. "The smell's so strong it might' nigh picks you up off your feet and carries you out over the stockade."

Stephanie turned and looked at the spring, noticing for the first time the ooze of black, smelly mire churned up by countless hoofs, and refuse thrown carelessly into the water to rot.

"Well," she said, sniffing from a safe distance, "it doesn't smell exactly like our house in the Back Country."

For a minute she was homesick for the clean spicy

scent of Bertha's herbs and barks and roots drying about the chimney—pennyroyal and horse mint, catnip and sarsaparilla and horehound, sassafras and spignet. No, she realized, Bertha Venable would never abide for any length of time such a smell as Harrod's Fort reeked of.

"Mammy's particular about the folks, too," Rob reported. "Says the families may be all right, but the outlandish menfolks that are here buyin' up the land ain't our kind. Says the fastest we can get on to our own claim and get it surveyed, and build a cabin on it ain't fast enough."

"What did Pappy 'low to that?" asked Stephanie.

"He's skittish about all these land grabbers, too, Pappy is. He's goin' to feel safer, he says, once he gets his hands on the surveyor's deed. But he told Mammy she wouldn't feel so high an' mighty about the Fort if the red men started raidin'."

"And Mammy?"

"Mammy says she's a-reservin' to herself the right to change her mind," said Rob. "But unless she's mighty mistaken, she ain't fortin'. Nosiree! One night's cured her."

The deputy surveyor paid no attention to the fact that Bertha had worked herself into a sweat trying to shake the dust of Harrod's Fort from her feet. He'd seen folks in a hurry before to get to their land. From the way they were pouring into Kentucky from every direction, he'd likely see a lot more before all of Kentucky County had been passeled out.

The dew was off the grass, and the wooded hollows were drenched with warm sunshine before the Venables finally filed out of the stockade and turned southwestward, Jonathan heading the line, with Stephanie at his heels. Behind Stephanie strode the deputy, leading his horse.

Stephanie, Rob, and Noel had fastened wide eyes on the deputy as he made ready for his day's work. Into the saddle bags now across the back of the horse he had packed the instruments of his trade. In one side was his compass, carefully wrapped and fitted into a box. In the other side were his tally pins, each with a strip of bright red linsey tied through the ring, a batch of rings made of deerskin whangs to slip on his belt at every tally measure, a chisel and a timber scribe, a hatchet, a whetstone, a steel punch, and a rat-tail file. With the compass the deputy had packed away some clean pages of paper, his goose quill pen, and some pokeberry ink. Back of the saddlebags were his heavy, gangly-linked surveyor's chains.

The deputy strode through the woods like a critter born to them. Only one of his surveyor's tools, his iron-shod jacob staff, he carried in his hand. In his belt he fastened an ax with which, on occasion, he slashed at undergrowth and grapevines to clear the way through the woods. In the bosom of his worn old shirt he carried some corn pone and jerk to stay his hunger if other food failed him. On his back was slung his long rifle. And in his head he carried a tongue loose at both ends.

Listening to his tales, thought Stephanie, was like watching Grandmammy Linney piece a quilt. Grandmammy, the winter before she died, took a heap of French scraps she'd saved of every color of the rainbow, and when she sewed them together and embroidered them with fancy French stitches, she had as pretty a crazy quilt as ever body set eyes on. The deputy took tales of every subject a body could imagine—bears and beavers, bald eagles and snow geese, copperheads and bullfrogs, log rollings and the Christmas shindig at the Fort on Corn Island where folks drank their fill of sling and danced the scamperdown and the double-shuffle till daylight—and when he got them all told and embroidered with his own fancy notions, he had Kentucky. And it was no more like Jonathan's plain Kentucky of fine black land than a dusky, green-spotted, wide-winged moth was like the cocoon that cabined it.

Whenever there was a lull in the deputy's talk, Jonathan turned to ply him with questions. Didn't a cornpatch claim to Kentucky land like his'n outweigh every other sort of claim? Would there be enough land for all the folks emptying into Kentucky County?

The deputy knew all the answers, Stephanie soon learned. But out of his answers sprouted a new crop of questions—nettlesome questions that pricked her lively pleasure in this broad, rolling land of plenty, that dimmed her eyes to the yellow trout lilies dancing above their spotted leaves, and dulled her ears to the mortal sweet song the birds were spilling out over the rim of the dark woods. She wished Noel could be up front in the line so that he could listen to the deputy's talk. Noel would lap it up like whipped sillabub. He'd know what to make of it all, too.

"Any red men been hereabouts lately?" asked Jonathan.

"Not down this way to speak of," the deputy said, hacking his way through the underbrush while beady-eyed squirrels stared at him in astonishment from arching branches overhead. "They're stayin' pretty well on their side of the Ohio since Colonel Clark showed 'em at Kaskasky and Cahoky out in the Illinois country what a whuppin' he's laid up for 'em if ever they set foot on Kentucky soil again."

"Governor Jefferson, looks like he showed good sense gettin' the Virginny legislature to pass that Land Law," said Jonathan.

Yes, agreed the deputy, Tom Jefferson was a smart man all right. The Virginia Land Law, passed the year before, in 1779, giving corn-patch claimants like Jonathan a title to their land was meant, first of all, to pour a little money into the Virginia treasury, said the deputy. Virginia was drained as dry as a creek bottom in a droughty year, carrying on more than her share of the war against England. The Land Law meant to be fair and square to everybody who wanted to settle on Virginia's waste and unappropriated lands in Kentucky County, of course, said the deputy, but there were sharpsters a-plenty loose in the world who were willing to do both Virginia and the corn-patch claimants out of their land.

Take the Transylvania Company, said the deputy. The Transylvania Company hired Daniel Boone to hack out a wilderness road and build a big fort at the mouth of Otter Creek. Then they called in delegates from all the Kentucky settlements—called it a convention—and wrote out a passel of rules for folks to go by. If it hadn't been for George Rogers Clark, who had a nose like a bloodhound for smelling out trouble, the Transylvania Company would have slipped a rope in the shape of British-smelling quitrents about the neck of every settler coming into Kentucky. But lucky for Jonathan Venable, and everybody else wanting to claim Kentucky land as free men, Clark got on to the wildcat schemes of the Transylvanians and cooked their goose with the Virginia legislature. George Rogers Clark was a smart man, he said. A mighty smart man, if he could keep his head.

But the Transylvania Company was just a drop in a piggin to all the speculators in the world who at that minute were making sheep's eyes at Kentucky, said the deputy. One company had been organized in England to grab up Kentucky land, he said. Another land company up in New York was doing its dead level best to persuade the Continental Congress to pass a law requiring Virginia to give up her western lands. Did anybody need to ask why? Hardly, said the deputy. While Virginia was down on her knees in a financial way, it was a mighty good time for New York to do her out of her western lands. And who could blame New York? There wasn't a man living who wouldn't like to cut himself off a slice of rich western lands. Hadn't old Ben Franklin and his boy tried to get a grant of western lands north of the Ohio a few years before? And George Washington—wasn't he pretty well fixed? And Patrick Henry. Governor Henry had himself fixed for life with all his western lands. He himself, the deputy said, had pre-empted a thousand acres and was saving for more.

"Looks like Tom Jefferson, since he took over the governorship, has set out to reform the whole system," said the deputy.

"All I ask of him, I reckon," said Jonathan, "is that he let folks alone. Jist let ever' feller govern hisself."

"That's all mighty fine," warned the deputy, "as long as things run along to suit folks. But let people head into trouble, and right away they begin to wonder, where's the government. And between you and me, Venable, Kentucky's likely to see a heap of trouble before ever'body's got the piece of black land he thinks is a-comin' to him. Ever' patch of land I survey, seems like I spy another loophole in that Land Law."

"Money scarce through here?" asked Jonathan.

The deputy halted at a branch flowing through the woods.

"Depends on what you mean when you say 'money,'" he said, as he waited for his horse to drink. "If you mean that Continental currency they're coinin' at Philadelphy, the woods is full of that paper. But it won't buy a thing. Not a dawgone thing. One dollar specie in Kentucky today's wuth five hundred dollars Continental paper money. I reckon the Virginny legislature was pretty smart when it said this Kentucky land had to be paid for in hard specie. I hear over in North Caroliny where you come from a feller has to take Continental money if it's offered him in exchange, else he's considered an enemy to the country and dealt with accordin'. Folks are runnin' away from their debtors, I hear, to keep from havin' to accept the wuthless paper."

"I reckon hit ain't quite that bad," Jonathan told him. "Though hit was bad enough when we left, an' worsenin' by the day."

"Feller in here from New Bern just last week said the North Caroliny legislature's talkin' of raisin' the tax rate to twelve pence a pound valuation in that state," said the deputy, "and levyin' all sorts of special taxes on single men, and slaves, and Dunkards and Mennonites and Quakers."

"I ain't heard that," said Jonathan.

"Said North Caroliny hadn't been able to keep her delegates in the Congress at Philadelphy except by fits and starts, because the treasury's as empty as a young un's stockin' the day after Christmas. And North Caroliny's the cow's tail when it comes to payin' for this war."

"I reckon hit is," agreed Jonathan.

"Ain't much British money left through here," the deputy went on. "Now, if you're lookin' for real money that'll stand anybody's acid," he added, reaching into his shirt bosom and taking out a pouch, "you want this here coin." He held up a Spanish milled dollar.

"Some of these others ain't so bad, either," he said, as he emptied the pouch into his palm and displayed one at a time a Portuguese Joe and a Half Joe, a Spanish doubloon and a pistoreen, and two silver wedges of coin. "This here's the new Kentucky currency," he laughed, holding up one of the wedges. "We needed change, so folks took to dividin' Spanish dollars into eight bits for change. These two bits are wuth quarter of a Spanish milled dollar.

"Looks like the Spanish have got the soundest money circulatin'," he went on. "And the soundest government, judgin' by the way their empire's spreadin' like fire in a canebrake all up along the Mississippi since they took over from the French. Money's like a pulse. You can always tell if a government's healthy or ailin' by what its money'll buy in the market. And when you try passin' off some of that Continental paper in Kentucky, you learn double quick how bad off the Continental Congress is. It's campin' in the buryin' ground, I'd say, with one foot danglin' in a bury hole."

"Any chance of a feller pre-emptin' a thousand acres of land before hit's all gone?" asked Jonathan. "Or the price skyrockets?"

"It all depends," said the deputy, clucking to his horse as Jonathan cut out through the woods again, "on whether or not you can scare up four hundred dollars specie to pay into the Virginny treasury. That's the government price for a thousand acres. Any feller that can lay his hands on four hundred dollars somewhere, and swap it for Kentucky land, 'll be mighty rich some day. But a body can't just beat four hundred dollars of anybody's money—British or Spanish or even Continental—out of the bushes. If you had corn to sell now, Venable, you'd strike it mighty rich. Feller come into the Fort last week with five bushels of corn and sold it for two hundred dollars a bushel. Folks nearly scalped him, they was that starved for bread. Happen to know old Tilly Balance out your way? Lonesome Tilly, folks call him."

"Heard of him," said Jonathan.

How queer, thought Stephanie, that her pappy had never mentioned to the Venables that they were to have neighbors in Kentucky.

"Some say he's hexed," said the deputy. "One feller come into the Fort t'other day and said he'd seen

Lonesome Tilly crossin' Salt River on steppin' stones nobody else could find. And another said he seen him one day runnin' along in the tops of trees for all the world like a squirrel. And Jim Snodgrass, he says he's seen Lonesome Tilly charm a rattlesnake till its rattles was as limber as water. But I've never heard tell that he put a spell on anybody. Just quare. Quare as a buzzard squattin' out here in the woods by his lonesome. Don't say a solitary word. You say there's a spring on your land, Venable?"

"Right down close to the river," said Jonathan.

"We might as well begin surveyin' there," announced the deputy. "A spring's a sort of natural landmark."

On through the woods they went, the warm, still air of May close about them. Stephanie, trudging along, busied herself with trying to ferret out the reasons why her pappy, after his summers in Kentucky, had harped all the time on the blackness and the fatness of the land, and had said so little about the sullying shadows that crisscrossed it like crow tracks crisscrossing new-fallen snow. But her pappy had never had a nose for smelling out trouble before he got to it, Stephanie realized.

Shadows or no shadows, however, land sharpsters and red men or no, Kentucky was every jot and tittle as fine a place as Jonathan had claimed, she could plainly see. The air was heavy with the sweet, heady smell of wild grapes in bloom. Pawpaw trees and hickory nut trees and chestnut trees were everywhere, and never would the Venables go hungry, if a body could believe all the tales the deputy told of turkey flocks so huge they blotted out the sun when they flew, of bears and deer and elk so thick they trampled one another down. And as for buffaloes, there were so tarnal many of them critters, the deputy said, that some folks shot them just for the hump, and some for the tongue, and some for no reason at all but to see if they could hit a target in the eye, and left the rest a-lying for the buzzards and the carrion crows.

But it wasn't going to be the pleasantest thing in the world, Stephanie reckoned, having a hexed old man living on the edge of the Venable claim.

4. Deed to the Land

A LITTLE LESS than two hours by the sun after leaving Harrod's Fort, Jonathan Venable came to a sudden stop.

"Well, folks," he announced, "here's the Venable claim. Here's whar I cleared for my corn patch two years back."

Stephanie set her kettle down and looked about her, a qualmish feeling boiling up in her stomach, as if she had lost her foothold and had turned a somersault off one of the high Appalachian peaks. This wasn't the

Garden of Eden she had brought herself to imagine after seeing how her pappy's plain, homespun words in praise of Kentucky needed a passel of embroidery stitches to make them match the wide, bouqueted earth. This was nothing but a little bitty square of land crowded on every side by ancient oaks and popples, choked with sprouts and whips and tall weeds, and with little to bear witness to Jonathan's sojourn in the land except a few girdled trees.

"Who made corn in the year 1778," the surveyor had read from the warrant. The Land Commissioners had set great store by that corn planting, making it the cornerstone of Jonathan's right to the land. But nowhere was there a sign of the unharvested crop.

"Well, Berthy?" said Jonathan.

For a minute Bertha stood at the edge of the clearing, gazing at the river that showed through the tree butts on the west, locating the spot where a spring bubbled out of the ground.

"It's a good place, Jonathan," she said, after a long time. "It's a mighty good place."

Jonathan's face lighted up with pleasure, as if he had known Bertha had a right to carp and carry on if she took a mind to. But her mammy, Stephanie guessed, must be seeing more than lay before her eyes. She had the de Monchard knack of making something out of nothing. Apt as not, in her mind she was building a fine house on the edge of that tangled thicket like the house of the circuit judge in Hillsborough. She was clearing fields as far as the eye would be able to see when all the trees were cut down, planting long rows of corn in the hollers, and pasturing sheep on sunny, grassy hillsides. She was hacking out a road past the house. She was having kinfolks come to Sunday dinner.

"I'm powerful glad you favor hit, Berthy," said Jonathan.

"I been all up and down this river," spoke up the deputy, "and you can take my word for it. Ain't nobody got a finer claim in Kentucky County than this right here."

"Well," announced Jonathan brusquely, "time's a-flyin'. I'll help the deputy with the surveyin'. Ought to get that out of the way first."

"Can I help, too?" begged Rob.

"I could sure make use of a boy like you to help with the tallyin'," said the deputy to Rob.

"If hit makes the surveyin' go quicker," considered Jonathan, "all right, Rob. Noel. . . ."

Jonathan looked out over his wild clearing, then at the creels into which were crammed the tools for taming it. He drew a long breath.

"Noel, you begin makin' handles," he said. "Better shape up the grubbin' hoe first. Then Steffy can begin choppin' out the bushes while your mammy gets her bearin's an' sets up housekeepin'. Begin cuttin' down them girdled trees, Noel. A cabin'll have to wait a spell, I reckon, till we get the land cleared an' corn in the ground. We been sleepin' under the stars a long time now. I reckon we can sleep that way a few nights more 'thout harm overtakin' us."

The deputy started down the wooded slope toward the spring, Rob, glad to be let off from chopping and grubbing, traipsing after him, Jonathan following Rob.

"Willie," Jonathan called back, "you stir your stumps, too. Soon as Noel gets a handle in the goose neck hoe, you start choppin' weeds and sprouts. Some things may be scarce in Kentucky," he added, "but one of 'em ain't choppin'."

Stephanie wished her pappy had picked Noel to help with the surveying. Noel looked at the deputy's instruments out of hungry eyes that would have been hungrier still had he but heard the deputy's flow of talk all the way from the Fort. She imagined the questions with which Noel would surely have plied the deputy could Jonathan have seen fit to send him instead of Rob tramping about the Venable claim, carrying the chains, studying the compass, sticking tally pins in the ground, scribing signs and initials on beech trees, marking witness corners.

As soon as Noel got a stout hickory handle fitted into the grubbing hoe, Stephanie started to work, chopping away at sprouts and vines, at waterweeds and nettles. But Bertha had need of Noel before he could begin chopping down trees. He'd have to shoot some squirrels for dinner, she said. And then he'd have to fetch his flint and tinder box and kindle her a fire.

The sun shone directly down on the abandoned corn patch when at last the squirrels were broiled, and the Venables sat on a fallen tree butt picking the meat from the little bones.

"Mammy, when can we have bread?" piped up Willie.

It had been more than a week since the last of the meal had been dusted out of the bag in which it had been carried. The last part of the journey among the foothills the Venables ate parched corn for bread, and acorns. Twice Bertha had sent the young uns to look in the black mud along the back water of a creek for the thick roots of the arrow-leaved wappatoo. These they stuck on sticks and roasted over the fire, and ate in place of bread.

Willie's face, Stephanie noticed, was growing peaked and pasty for lack of bread. So was Rob's. Many a time on the journey Rob had complained of a pain in his stomach. Then Bertha had set him to looking for spicy, spindle-shaped ginseng roots to chew.

"It takes a sight of time to make bread," Bertha told Willie, patiently, "and a passel of hands. First, we'll have to get this clearin' in plantin' shape, and that'll take Noel cuttin' down trees, and Steffy grubbin' sprouts, and you diggin' up weeds a matter of three days, I reckon. Barrin' bad weather. A sight of weather, good, bad, and indifferent, goes into bread, too."

"What're Rob and Pappy goin' to do?" asked Willie. "Will the surveyin' take all summer?"

"That won't take more than a day, I reckon," Bertha told him. " 'Bout dark, Rob and your pappy'll be home with a deed. Then they'll help with the clearin'. But there's only one ax, and only one grubbin' hoe, and only one goose neck hoe. And the wilderness is eternal great big against one ax, one grubbin' hoe, and one goose neck hoe.

"But never mind," she consoled Willie. " 'Bout Monday, after Noel gets handles fitted into the plow, your pappy'll hitch up Job and break this new ground the best he can in between the stumps. Then he'll get him a thorn tree and put logs on it and let Job drag it around to harrow the ground. Then Steffy'll dig holes, and you and Cassie can drop corn in 'em. You'll have to be mighty careful not to lose a solitary kernel. Every kernel means a hoecake. You'll drop three kernels in every hill. Then Steffy'll come along with the hoe and cover 'em up."

"And then they'll come up, and grow big, and then we'll have bread," said Willie, his eyes shining in his lean face.

"But not so all-fired fast as that," said Noel, stretching on his back to rest.

Bertha took a strip of bark and raked ashes over the live coals to keep the seed of the fire Noel had kindled.

"Not till the sun and the rain do their work, Willie," she said. "It takes a heap of sun and rain, workin' at corn sprouts, to turn 'em into bread. A body mustn't ever forget he can't raise corn all by hisself, but has to have the sun and the rain to help him.

"And while the sun and the rain are doin' their work, us Venables'll have to do ours," Bertha told him. "Rob and Steffy'll have to keep the sprouts and the weeds chopped out so the young corn can push its roots deep into the ground. And you and Cassie'll have to sit out here in the clearin', day after day after day, and scare varmints and squirrels and crows away."

"That long, Mammy?" pleaded Willie.

"It takes a sight of patience on the part of humans to make bread," Bertha told him. "Even after the corn's laid by, and there's no more work for humans to put their hands to in the corn patch, they still have to wait. And wait. And waitin's lots harder than workin'. But by and by, one mornin' you'll find a cornstalk puttin' out gold tassels at the top, and spillin' red silks out of an ear shapin' up in a middle joint. Finer than gold and red banners of fine French silks and velvets belongin' to a King Louis."

"And then we'll have bread!" cried Willie.

"Then, in a week or so, about the end of July, when the corn is in the milk, we'll have roastin' ears," said Bertha. "I calculate we can spare two messes of roastin' ears from the patch. Then we'll have to wait some more till the milk in the kernels thickens and the kernels begin to dry and harden."

"And then we'll have bread?" asked Willie.

"Then we'll have mush," said Bertha. "We'll scrape some of the ears, and boil the kernels in the kettle, and season 'em with fat from the bear your pappy's goin' to kill, and we'll have us a mess of mush. And then we'll have to wait a little longer."

"Much longer?"

"Till frost is in the air. Till the blue geese are honkin' south, and the oaks are firin' up. Till Noel gets me a hominy block hollered out, and fixes me up a pestle for poundin' the kernels."

"And then we'll have bread!" shouted Willie.

"Then we'll have bread!" echoed Bertha. "And we'll have vittles to eat with it—taters to roast in the ashes, and shucky beans to boil with side meat, reckonin' the bears let our pigs grow up. And we'll have venison that your pappy brings home from the woods, and walnuts and hickory nuts and chinquapins that you and Cassie bring home from the hollers. And we'll maybe have honey, if we find a bee tree Noel can rob. And Steffy'll gather elderberries, and I'll make some cordial for special days like your birthday."

Willie sat straight on the log, his eyes dancing.

Stephanie shut her eyes to keep from seeing him. She tried to shut out of her mind, too, the image of such tasty vittles. The thought of them only mocked a body sitting there in the midst of nothing. She threw away the bone she was picking and got to her feet.

"But don't forget, there's a sight of work between the Venables and bread, young uns," said Bertha. "We'd best be at it."

For an hour Stephanie grubbed at stubborn roots while Noel chopped away at a big, girdled popple. Already Stephanie had blisters on her palms from the rough hoe handle.

In the middle of the afternoon she and Noel went down the hill to the spring. Stephanie doused her face in the cold, clear water, made a cup of her hands and drank from it, and cooled her hot, tired, dusty feet in the rill.

"Did you hear what the deputy was tellin' Pappy this mornin'?" she asked, as Noel flopped on his stomach and drew water into his mouth in long, cooling sups, like a thirsty horse.

"No, what?" he brought up his dripping chin to ask.

As they rested in the shade of the trees, everything she could remember about Indians, about North Carolina taxes, about black Kentucky land that a body would almost part with his soul to own, about the sorry state of the Continental Congress and the Congress' money, about Lonesome Tilly Balance, word for word, Stephanie told him.

What Noel thought about these things he kept to himself.

"Noel," asked Stephanie, plucking a sprig of the wild

mint that fringed the spring and nibbling at the leaves, "what makes people hexed?"

"They lose their bearin's," said Noel.

"Are they born that way?"

"Sometimes," said Noel. "Sometimes not."

"Then what happens to make 'em hexed?" asked Stephanie. "What do you reckon happened to Lonesome Tilly Balance?"

"Deputy said he squatted out here all by his self, didn't he?" reminded Noel. "Been out here all by his lonesome four or five years maybe. Maybe longer. No folks around. Ain't that enough to cause a body to lose his bearin's? How'd you like to live in these woods by your lonesome?" he asked.

Stephanie shivered.

"Know what Uncle Lucien says?" asked Noel. "He says it's bein' afraid that makes people hexed, that makes 'em lose their bearin's. Everybody that's afraid's a little bit hexed, 'cause he's lost his bearin's just so much."

"Are you afraid, Noel?" Stephanie asked.

"Not specially. As long as I'm not taken unawares, I'm not specially afraid. And I don't mean to be taken unawares."

"Not even of red men, are you afraid?"

"Not even of red men."

"Not even of the British?"

"Not even of the British."

"Not even of Lonesome Tilly?"

"Shucks, naw, Steffy. The more hexed a man is, if he ain't plumb daft, the more he hankers for a little human kindness. If ever you meet up with him, just say 'Howdy' natural like. Don't run away from him."

The sun was setting when Jonathan and Rob came back from their surveying.

"Deputy says my deed'll be all fixed up in due time," Jonathan announced, proud as a royal governor. "I 'low hit'll be a matter of three or four days. Somebody'll have to go to the Fort to get hit. Now, all we have to do is to get our crops out, an' build us a cabin, an' hunt enough to stave off starvation till the corn's ripe."

The Venables slept that night on pallets of pine boughs which Bertha and Willie gathered and banked against a near-by wooded knoll. Squirrel meat was their supper—squirrel meat and the milk that ought to come a little higher in the piggin at milking time, now that Brownie's long, hard journey was over and she could forage her fill on buffalo grass and pea vine and young cane growing in the river bottom.

For three days, from early to late, Jonathan and Noel chopped away at the dead trees. They wrapped log chains around the straightest trunks and with the help of Job snaked them to the edge of the clearing to be used in building the cabin. The limbs and the brush Noel and Stephanie heaped in a great mound in the middle of the clearing, and burned in a roaring, booming, crackling, snapping fire.

At the end of a week, Jonathan looked proudly over the clearing, dotted with stumps, and planted with the seed brought from the Back Country—corn and beans, potatoes and gourds and pumpkins.

"I reckon a body ought to start raisin' a cabin tomorrow," he said. "But 'twouldn't be a bad notion to get my deed first. Noel, you an' Steffy go in to the Fort tomorrow an' see if the deputy's got the deed all writ out. Don't know as a body need get in a swivet over hit," he added, by way of excusing his haste, "but I reckon I'll breathe easier when I get my hands on them papers. Me an' Rob'll go buffalo huntin'."

In the early morning, Noel and Stephanie set out toward Harrod's Fort, along the trail they had traveled so short a time before, using as guide marks the slashes the deputy had made in the undergrowth. Noel walked in front, carrying his rifle. Stephanie trudged barefoot behind him, her eyes always watching the woods for a sign of moving things.

The Fort, they found, was restless with people coming and going, just as it had been when the Venables arrived from the Back Country. It was sure a sight to see the flatboats on the Ohio, folks said. Looked like there'd be nobody left at Fort Pitt, if people kept coming to Kentucky at this rate. And folks were pouring out of

Virginia and the Carolinas like water out of a pitcher spout, grabbing up Kentucky land like it was a hoecake in the wilderness, they said.

"Howdy, young uns," said the surveyor when he spied Noel and Stephanie standing in the doorway of the blockhouse. The deputy was nowhere about. "What you after?"

"Pappy's deed," said Noel. "Is it ready?"

"Jonathan Venable's deed? Why, no, son. That land was just surveyed. Just a week ago," said the surveyor.

"But Pappy thought the deed might be ready," Noel explained. "The deputy told him 'in due time.' Pappy sent us to see."

"Don't your pappy know the law on that?" asked the surveyor, frowning at Noel.

"I reckon not," said Noel. "What is the law?"

"Why, he can't get his deed till December," said the surveyor. "That's accordin' to the law. That's to give the Land Court a chance to hear all rival claims that may be entered on the same tract, you see. Now, if no caveat is entered against your pappy's land, in December the Land Court'll make out his deed and his title's clear. But if anybody else claims the same tract of land, and registers that claim with the Court of Commissioners before December 1, the court'll have to decide to which party to award the land."

The surveyor spoke kindly enough to Noel, but his words chilled Stephanie to the marrow. She turned them over in her mind, trying to change their meaning, trying to find in them some certainty to cling to. But a law like that was clear and cold as ice, she reckoned, and not a great comfort to a body who had just planted his last kernel of corn in a clearing in exchange for which he had given most of his worldly goods.

"Is it likely anybody else'll claim Pappy's land?" she heard Noel asking.

"Every day, son, somebody turns up claimin' somebody else's land under old royal grants of some sort or another," the surveyor said. "All we can do is to enter all claims, survey them, and decide who comes first. We try to play no favorites."

Stephanie's legs felt weak under her. She turned to go, but Noel had one more question to put to the surveyor.

"Is there a copy of the Land Law hereabouts?" he asked.

"No closer than Williamsburg, I reckon," said the surveyor.

"I—I thought I'd like to read it," explained Noel.

The surveyor smiled at him. "Can you read?" he asked.

"Some," said Noel.

"Well, I reckon you'll have to go to Williamsburg to read the Land Law," said the surveyor. "But tell your pappy to go right ahead plantin' his crops. 'Tain't likely anybody'll try to oust him. When it comes to a showdown in these parts between old royal claims and corn roots in the ground, the corn roots can outtalk the royal claims mighty nigh every time."

Noel had no fine words to say to the surveyor in exchange for his heartening advice, but as he turned to go, a warmth kindled by the surveyor's kindness spread over his slim face.

"Say!" called the surveyor after Noel. He got up from the three-legged puncheon stool on which he sat and came and leaned against the door jamb. "You got any books to read?" he asked.

"No," said Noel. "Nary a one."

"Would you like to have one?" asked the surveyor.

Stephanie glanced at Noel. Why, that was what he was hankering after, she decided. Books. At the mention of books, he looked like a body who has been starved to skin and bones drawing up his stool to plenty. His whole face lighted up from the roots of his sun-bleached hair to his neck, and light flooded his eyes and washed away the sullenness and the lonesomeness.

"Have you—got a book?" Noel asked.

"No," said the surveyor. "But a preacher feller came through here last week. Stayed all night here at the Fort on his way to his claim over close to Stoner's. He had three or four books with him—a Bible, and George Fox's *Journal*, and Barkley's *Apology*, and *Pilgrim's Progress*. Tell you what I'll do. I'll ask him if he comes over this way again to bring you a book. When you come in to the Fort you can pick it up, then bring it back when you finish."

Noel stood tongue-tied. Stephanie nudged his arm.

"I'm sure—I'm sure much obliged," Noel muttered.

"Not at all," said the surveyor. "And tell your pappy not to worry."

Hurriedly Noel and Stephanie turned and walked across the square and through the big gates of the stockade, no longer paying mind to land speculators and land-hungry families and their comings and goings and doings. Outside the Fort they began to run as fast as Noel could run with a long rifle on his shoulder, never stopping for breath until they were deep within the woods.

"Reckon what book the preacher feller'll bring, Noel?" asked Stephanie, sensing that the notion was almost too grand to be bandied about in words.

"Maybe *Pilgrim's Progress,*" said Noel. "I'd sure like *Pilgrim's Progress.* Uncle Lucien told me about that one."

It was like a secret that they took from some hiding place and looked at for a minute, then hid away again. Not another word did they say about the book.

"I sure wish we had a deed, carryin' it to Pappy," said Stephanie after a while. "He's goin' to be mighty uneasy when we tell him what the surveyor said."

"He'll worry till he gets his hands on the deed, for certain," agreed Noel. "But supposin' the surveyor had given us a deed, Steffy. It ain't so simple as that."

"What d'you mean, Noel?" she asked, feeling afraid. Noel carried dark knowledge in his head, always, she reflected.

"Do you know who owns this land, Steffy?" asked Noel.

"Virginny, of course," she said.

"And the Virginny legislature passes a Land Law statin' on what terms a man can buy Kentucky County land, and how much he has to pay for it. We'll even say nobody else claims Pappy's land, and he gets a deed to it. All right. But how did Virginny come by the land?"

"Virginny—Virginny's always had it," said Stephanie, not quite sure of her ground. "His Majesty granted it to her."

"That's just it," said Noel. "His Majesty granted it to her. But what's to keep His Majesty from takin' it back, if he wins this war? If the British win this war, Steffy, His Majesty and not the Virginny legislature'll tell Pappy what he can have and what he can't have. His Majesty'll tell Pappy how much he's goin' to be taxed and what little he can keep for himself. He'll tell Pappy when to bow and scrape before his bigwigs, and we'll never get our chance to know what it's like to be free and to make our own laws and run our own government. That's why

I wanted to join Marion, Steffy," he confided. "That's why I want to join him more than ever now. There ain't many men seein' straight in this country right now. Don't you know that's what the deputy's talk added up to?"

They walked a long way in silence before Noel spoke again.

"Folks are too busy scandalizin' the Continental Congress," he said. "They're all tryin' to get their hands on hard Spanish money. They're grabbin' up Kentucky land while it's cheap, but doin' precious little to keep it free. Folks are too blind, Steffy, and too scared. They're a little hexed, a lot of 'em are. And not one in a hundred of 'em, I reckon, has ever thought what it'd be like if we win our chance. Or, for that matter, if we lose it."

Fear settled heavily on Stephanie. In the Back Country she had occasionally picked up a scrap of talk that terrorized her. Savannah taken by the British . . . houses looted . . . patriots shot . . . Old Man Carpenter standing and shaking his head when British soldiers tried to make him take the oath of allegiance to His Majesty. . . . Old Man Carpenter hanged. . . . Cornwallis bringing three thousand men from New York. . . . Cornwallis pounding at the defenses of Charleston.

Now Noel's talk terrified her in the same way.

"What'll happen to us, Noel?" she asked.

"I don't know," he said. "Nobody knows. I only know Kentucky ain't free yet, not for all the warrants in the blockhouse."

"Can we do somethin' about it?" she begged him.

"Some day," he promised her. "Wherever people are chained, there'll come a chance some day to break the chains, I reckon. That's what Uncle Lucien says."

"Whenever that chance comes, Noel—"

"Whenever it comes close enough, I'm a-goin'," said Noel.

Stephanie felt suddenly very proud of him. The faith with which she believed in him was every whit as stout as the faith with which he believed in Francis Marion, and in the cause for which Marion, under orders from General Washington, commanded a few stragglers who believed, while most of the world doubted.

"Whenever the time comes for you to go, Noel," she promised, "I'll help you."

5. Lonesome Tilly

LONG BEFORE sunup the next morning the Venables rose from their pine bough pallets, stretched themselves, and set to work. Noel went to the edge of the clearing to call up the pigs and the chickens, to count the sheep, and unhobble the horse.

Some day they would fence in a pasture for the critters, said Jonathan. And after a year or two when they could raise enough corn to fatten pigs, they'd build a rail pen to keep the troublesome hogs in at night. Until the Venables got a shelter over their own heads, however, and vittles on their table, dumb animals would have to run free and forage through the woods. But their freedom was as studded with danger as a skunk cabbage was studded with spots.

As long as the wolves had plenty of deer for breakfast, dinner, and supper, and baby fawns for light snacks between meals, Jonathan reckoned the sheep would be safe. But nobody could tell when a bear might pounce on one of the pigs, wrap him in his forelegs, and make off with him, running like a man, through the woods. The deputy said he once saw a bear running two-legged that way, toting a wriggling pig in his forelegs faster than a man could follow.

Stephanie untethered Brownie and milked her in a corner of the clearing. She sighed with relief as the last of the pigs came loping in answer to Noel's "Sho, pig! Sho, pig! Pig! Pig! Pig!" and turned her thoughts to other matters.

"I aim to plant my apple seed today," she told Noel.

"Whereabouts?" he asked.

"I haven't decided," Stephanie told him.

"Grandmammy's tree was planted right beside the door of their old house," Noel told her. "It was bloomin' when I left Charleston. Steppin' outside the door was like steppin' out into a perfumed cloud. And the bees were poppin' in and out of that tree like popcorn."

"My tree'll bloom that way, too," said Stephanie. "It sure will be a pretty sight, won't it, bloomin' here in the wilderness every springtime? But I don't aim to call it 'The Tree of St. Jean de Maurienne,' " she added. "I aim to call it 'The Tree of Freedom.' Your kind of freedom."

"A Tree of Freedom's apt to grow bitter fruit," Noel told her. "Sometimes mighty costly fruit."

"I know," said Stephanie.

All the Venable young uns knew from Bertha the story of the bitter, costly apples Marguerite de Monchard's tree had borne.

When the de Monchards fled their country and their biggety king, Bertha told the Venable young uns, because they refused to forsake their religion and make slaves of their consciences, they thought it mighty poor grace to begin enslaving others as soon as they found refuge in a new world, as many of the Huguenots who had fled France before them had done. The de Monchards looked on with sickening heart as broad rice fields turned the simple holdings of their Huguenot neighbors into estates, as fashionable country seats strutted up where simple Huguenot cottages had stood.

Had the liberty-loving Huguenots tended the rice and swept the mansion floors with their own hands, well and good, Bertha said. But no, they bought black men and women off the auction block in Charleston. In time a Huguenot came to be known by the number of slaves he owned. Black gold, he called his slaves. The black men and women bent their backs in the hot, swampy rice fields, and swept the mansion floors, cooked the vittles, and shooed the flies off their Huguenot masters and mistresses, while the sting and the black sorrow of slavery seeped into them like a poison.

The de Monchards were a stubborn lot, Bertha told her young uns. Proud and stubborn. It was told of Marguerite that one day she and her pappy went walking through the Charleston market place, and heard an auctioneer's loud, raucous rigmarole, parading the salable qualities of a big Gambian Negro standing chained on the auction block. The Gambian was as strong as a brute ox for field labor, barked the auctioneer; he was docile; he had had the smallpox; he was already branded with two circles, one above the other, on his right buttock; he ought to bring not a shilling less than fifty pounds; if cash were offered, he might be had ten per cent cheaper, and rice and indigo might be used in place of specie.

Marguerite de Monchard was sixteen then. At that point in the transaction, it was told of her that she broke through the crowd of buyers and bystanders and, standing before the auctioneer, screamed at him that he was no better than the tyrant who ruled France, and that wherever he went, deep, black shame ought to go with him that he could traffic in human beings as if they were cattle.

Annoyed men, who couldn't hear the auctioneer's description of the Gambian above her outburst, caught her and handed her, furious and outraged, to her pappy. Slowly the two of them made their way out of the tittering crowd and across the market square, Marguerite sobbing as she went.

That night the de Monchards made an agreement. They would go to the slave market themselves the next morning, they decided, and pay in cash for as many slaves as their money would buy, and give such slaves their freedom.

It was a long story Bertha told the Venable young uns of the slaves whose freedom was purchased by the de Monchards. But in the end, Bertha said, the de Monchards got licked for their pains. When their money was gone, they found most of their friends gone, too, while the dent they had made in the institution of slavery was so little a body couldn't see it even with a spyglass trained on it. Then they packed up their belongings and started north in the direction of the Tar River in North Carolina, where, they had heard, freedom-loving folks called Quakers had settled. They would seek asylum and new fields to cultivate among the Quakers, they decided.

Lucien, however, stayed in the old home because he was keeping a school for boys in Charleston, and he had a notion he might deal slavery a few blows in the schoolroom. It was in the Quaker settlement on the Tar that

Grandmammy Marguerite had married Grandpappy Linney.

"Grandmammy's tree cost her a sight, I reckon," said Stephanie, picturing the sunny, pleasant French village of St. Jean de Maurienne which the de Monchards had had to flee, and the spacious, broad-verandahed South Carolina houses, the broad, low-lying rice fields, and the many black slaves on which they had turned their backs. "But Mammy's tree in the Back Country—it wasn't so costly."

"Sometimes freedom's like a light you have to keep a-tendin', day in, day out," Noel said. "Nobody tries specially to blow it out. But it gets dimmer and dimmer if somebody ain't always tendin' the oil. That's what Mammy's done. She's tended the oil. And the wick. Why do you think she dinged at Pappy all summer to let me have a little schoolin' when Preacher Craig norated around that he'd teach a school on the Waxhaw fall before last? And why do you think she outtalked Pappy, and sent me to Uncle Lucien last winter? Know what Governor Jefferson's doin'?" he asked. "Uncle Lucien says he's talkin' up free education for everybody."

"What's free education?" asked Stephanie.

"Schools where the scholars don't have to pay."

"But somebody has to pay," said Stephanie, recollecting the goose feathers Bertha had traded to Preacher Craig in exchange for Noel's brief schooling.

"Oh, everybody'll pay all right," Noel told her.

"Everybody that has property, that is. Property owners'll be taxed for free schools."

"Taxed?" said Stephanie. "Well, Pappy sure ain't goin' to take to that."

After breakfast, Stephanie took the grubbing hoe, and on the east edge of the clearing turned up leaf mold, and crumbled it with her fingers to make a cool, black bed in which to lay her apple seed.

"What you plantin'?" asked Willie.

"A Tree of Freedom," Stephanie told him.

"What kind of tree's a Tree of Freedom?" asked Willie.

"A tree that grows sometimes sweet apples, sometimes bitter ones," said Stephanie.

"Humph!" sniffed Willie. "You're gullin'."

That morning Jonathan began cutting down trees for the Venable cabin.

"Shucks, now!" he said, as he picked up his ax. "If a body jist had a passel of neighbors, we'd get this cabin up in three shakes of a sheep's tail."

Every Venable knew, however, that Jonathan would be skittish if he had enough neighbors to help raise a cabin. A few neighbors he liked, and after a long spell of lonesomeness, he warmed toward folks the way a freezing man warms toward a fire. But if, on some winter morning when all the leaves were off the trees, a body, by standing on a rise of ground, could look a far piece up the river and down the river, and see blue smoke curling from half a dozen chimneys, then Jonathan would likely begin to complain that he felt crowded. Then his feet would begin to itch, and nothing would cure the itching except a week's hunt in the woods by his lonesome, and looking out over wild country where no white man had ever set foot.

The Venables working by themselves could raise a cabin in a couple of weeks, but not the sort of cabin Bertha wanted. A puncheon floor Bertha wanted, and a window, a cockloft, and a chimney made of rocks.

To all these fancy notions Jonathan raised objections. First of all, it was a piece of foolishness, he said, to build so fine a cabin unless he had a deed to the land on which he aimed to build it. Then, there wasn't time to raise a regular Tidewater mansion, he told Bertha. Time was short, considering all a body had to do before winter overtook them. It was enough to get four walls up and a roof over their heads.

"And, besides," he added, "a puncheon floor's a hot-bed of splinters. The young uns'll be nussin' festered feet all winter."

"What are you aimin' to do with the skins from all the bears and buffaloes you aim to kill but lay 'em on the floor?" Bertha asked him.

"And a rock chimney!" Jonathan complained. "Mud and sticks are good enough for most chimneys around here, I notice."

"A rock chimney ain't tinder like a stick chimney," Bertha reminded him. "And anyway, it ain't as if the river bed wasn't choked with rocks to be had for the pickin' up."

Jonathan gave in grudgingly.

"You can leave the chinkin' out of the walls," Bertha said, thinking to lighten the labor of raising so fine a cabin with so few hands. "Fall will be time enough to daub the cracks, I reckon."

As long as they slept on the pine bough pallets and cooked their vittles in the clearing, it seemed to Stephanie they were only resting in their long, weary journey from the Back Country, and any morning they might reload Job and head west again. But the first log laid flush against the rectangle of earth which had been cleared of every kind of growth, and raked clean as a floor, was like a Venable taproot working its way down deep into the black Kentucky earth, and holding the Venables firmly in that spot.

With Jonathan and Noel taking turns, a *chop, chop, chop,* slow, but steady as the ticking of a clock, enlivened the words all day long, as the ax bit out of ancient tree butts great white chips smelling sweet of sap. Popple trees and oak trees Jonathan chose for the walls of the cabin, and oak for the floors, while he marked for shakes to cover the cabin a straight-grained oak whose bushy crown seemed to be brushing the clouds across the sky. Jonathan put Rob to work hacking the bark off the felled trees with a hatchet. Stephanie and Willie he sent to the river to hunt chimney rocks.

Willie wasn't a sight of help, but he filled out the letter of the wilderness law Jonathan and Bertha laid down for the Venable young uns. A young un under no circumstances was to go by his lonesome into the woods, Jonathan said. Never. Nor out of earshot of the clearing. Two must go together. There was no end of bears in the woods, and the wilderness could still hide red men. It didn't matter a piny woods Tory, said Bertha, how sure and certain a body was that the Indians had all been driven north of the Ohio, nor how much confidence the deputy placed in the man named George Rogers Clark. It paid to be cautious, at least as long as Clark was off traipsing about the Illinois country where the deputy said he was.

"Two sets of eyes are sharper than one," Bertha summed things up. "And two sets of ears are keener than one."

"But two sets of legs ain't faster than one, Mammy," Rob told her.

"What are your eyes and ears but leg-savin' devices?" she asked him.

Stephanie and Willie traipsed down the steep slope to the river and took a long look across to satisfy themselves that red men weren't hiding in the cane and the willows on the far bank.

"It's big, flat rocks we want, Willie," said Stephanie. "You be the spy and hunt 'em out, and I'll come along and capture 'em."

Along the river northward they went, Willie in front, wading in the shallow water along the bank, pointing out likely chimney stones. Stephanie waded after him, lugging to dry land such of his findings as appeared likely for a chimney, and piling them in a heap. Rob and Noel would carry the rocks up the hill when Jonathan was ready to build the chimney.

"How about knockin' off for a rest, Willie?" Stephanie asked, when she had built six piles of rocks.

The notion suited Willie.

"Right back there in the woods is a big patch of wintergreen," he said. "Pappy and I found it the other day. I'm goin' to get some for us to eat."

"You can't go by your lonesome," Stephanie told him.

"But it's right through there," he pointed. "You can might' nigh see it from here."

"Well," said Stephanie grudgingly. "I reckon. As long as we can still hear the ax. But don't be gone long. And holler if you want me."

Hardly had the big trees closed around Willie when Stephanie began to wish he had not gone. A body never could tell what lay in wait for little shavers in the woods. A whole passel of things might happen to a young un besides having red men steal him and carry him off and keep him the rest of his days, and leave his pappy and his mammy and all his kinfolks wondering right down to their bury holes what had become of him. A rattle-snake with eyes like red-hot coals of fire and a body rising and falling like a gunsmith's bellows, or a sluggish copperhead out looking for frogs, might fang him. A bear or a slinking wolf or a painter might make off with him. Eagles, too, folks said, sometimes swooped down and picked up young uns and flew straight to their nests in the tiptop of craggy mountains. The deputy said a bald eagle once, clean as a whistle, stole a little baby belonging to some folks settling on Otter Creek near Boone's Fort.

The sun was climbing high, Stephanie noticed. She sat on a big bald rock near the edge of the river with her feet dangling in the cool stream. The sun felt hot on her bare head. It warmed her tired shoulders through her cottonade dress, and made her sleepy.

"Steffy!"

From deep in the woods came Willie's voice, so faint and smothered Stephanie could scarcely hear it. She stiffened with fear. Goose bumps broke out on her arms as she got to her feet.

"Steff-ee! Come a-runnin'!"

Through the woods she stumbled, afraid to go, afraid not to go.

A stone's throw from the river she spied Willie, making himself little behind a tree at the edge of a bed of May apples. It was plain to see that whatever was wrong, he wasn't scared of anything.

When he saw her peeping through the undergrowth, he made signs for her to come to him.

"Looky!" he whispered, pointing to a near-by sycamore that stood dying of old age. "Up in that there hole. See?"

Stephanie stared upward at the hole, twenty feet above the ground.

"I don't see anything," she told him. She was about to tell him, too, not to scare her that way again, ever, as long as he lived, but he put his finger across his mouth as a warning to her to be quiet.

"Keep a-lookin'," he whispered.

Stephanie fastened her eyes on the hole and waited.

"Look out! She's a-comin'!" whispered Willie, his voice smaller and more excited than ever.

"I don't see a thing!" grumbled Stephanie.

"Sh-h-h! Look 'way up!" whispered Willie.

Down through the trees to a limb of the sycamore plummeted a mammy wood duck, a slim, gray-brown bird with eyes bugged out with caution.

"She shot out of that hole a while ago like a bullet," whispered Willie. "She's hidin' somethin' in there, I bet."

"Babies," whispered Stephanie.

"How do you know?"

"Because it's baby time."

Cocking her head on one side, then on the other, the skittish duck rose from the limb, sailed straight for the tree trunk, and dropped out of sight into the hole. In a minute she was out again, and on the ground, prancing around in the May apple bed, persuading in her high-pitched, wary, duck voice.

"Pee, pee, pee, pee, pee!"

Over and over she begged. Then she waited. Begged and waited.

"That's the way she was behavin' when I called you," Willie whispered, so low that Stephanie could scarcely make out the words he said. "I scared her, I reckon."

Stephanie, motionless, pursed her mouth as a sign to him to keep quiet. As still as shadows they stood, their bodies pressed close against the tree, waiting.

Up flew the duck. Into the hollow of the sycamore she darted, then out again. Once more she dropped to the ground among the May apples and pranced nervously about.

"Pee, pee, pee, pee, pee!"

As they waited, her skittishness left her and she stopped her prancing. Standing shyly among the May apples, she began calling again, this time more plaintively.

Stephanie nudged Willie. "Look in the hole!" she whispered.

High on the edge of the hole balanced a little bitty ball of down, blackish and yellowish, blinking its eyes at the big, green, shady world.

Willie leaned forward, but Stephanie held him back.

"It can't get down, Steffy!" whispered Willie, anxiety in his voice.

"You wait and see," Stephanie told him. "Little wild things can always make out. Just you be still and don't scare the little mite."

The baby duckling perched on the edge of the hole a minute, listening to its mammy, turning its downy head first to one side, then to the other. Then, all of a sudden, it gave itself a shove into space, flapped its little bitty wings as hard as it could, hit the ground, bounced like an India rubber ball, righted itself, and tore in a waddling run on its brand-new feet through the May apple bed toward its mammy.

"I'm goin' to catch it," whispered Willie. "I can have it for a pet, 'stid of a kitten."

"You got nothin' to feed it," said Stephanie. "Look! Here comes another."

A long time they waited, watching the hole while thirteen ducklings, one after the other, clambered to the edge of the hole, screwed up their courage to leap the long leap to the ground, and waddled after their mammy in the direction of the river.

"Help me catch just one, Steffy!" begged Willie.

"The little tykes don't like to be caught," she told him, coming out from behind the tree. "They're too tender. You better just get a coon for a pet, like Mammy said. And we both better get back to our rocks."

She squatted to pick some leaves of wintergreen growing on the other side of the tree, but with the dark, waxy leaves halfway to her mouth, she stopped short, her body taut as a bowstring as she noticed a slight movement among the bushes. Her feet froze to the ground with terror. Before she could leap through the May apple bed and run for her life, dragging Willie by the hand, a queer old man looking like some strange wild critter of the woods stepped out in full view.

Willie grabbed Stephanie around the knees and began to whimper.

"Hush!" she scolded, trying to think.

At least, she told herself above the wild thumping of her heart, the man wasn't an Indian. And he didn't carry a weapon—neither a knife, nor a rifle, nor a tomahawk.

As reason came slowly back to her, she noticed that the man wasn't a mite taller than Noel. His white hair that needed hackling fell about his shoulders, and his long dirty-white beard straggled down his chest. His arms and his feet were bare, and the few clothes he wore looked not so much like hunting shirt and breeches as a queer assortment of patches and tatters of varmint skin he had grown on himself. He stood staring first at Stephanie, then at Willie, with eyes as soft as a heifer's in his rusty face—eyes, Stephanie noticed, that seemed to have stayed young while the rest of him grew hoary.

Suddenly Stephanie remembered what Noel had told her: "When you meet up with Lonesome Tilly Balance, just say 'Howdy,' natural like."

She thought of the baby ducks screwing up their courage. Skittishly she screwed up her own.

"Howdy!" she managed to say, scarcely above a whisper.

The old man said never a word. He had his eyes fastened on Willie, and even when he turned and padded away, critter like, on his bare feet into the deep woods, he gazed over his shoulder at the young un until he was out of sight.

"Who was that, Steffy?" whimpered Willie, still clinging to her.

"That was Lonesome Tilly Balance," she told him, her voice quavery with fright.

Willie began to cry. "Will he hex us?" he asked.

"No. Don't you see you're not hexed?" she scolded. "He—he was just watchin' the ducks. Same as you. He likes ducks, apt as not."

"Where's he gone?"

"Home, I reckon."

"Where's his home?"

"Over yonder on his claim somewhere."

"What's he doin' on Pappy's claim then?" asked Willie. "These here are Pappy's trees. I don't want him to come here."

Leading Willie by the hand, Stephanie hurried toward the sound of the chopping, away from the river. She'd better tell her pappy about Lonesome Tilly, she decided.

"He didn't hurt anything, did he?" she asked, feeling braver as the sound of the chopping grew nearer.

"He might have," said Willie in a tearful voice,

crowding against Stephanie in his eagerness not to be left behind, and glancing fearfully over his shoulder now and then.

"But he didn't," Stephanie told him. "Don't go out huntin' for trouble, Willie. You can plague yourself to death that way. Like as not, Lonesome Tilly's as genteel as—as a high-born Tidewater gentleman, if you're genteel to him."

6. Visitors

JONATHAN rested his arms from chopping while he listened to Stephanie's tale of the queer old man she and Willie had come upon in the woods. Rob laid down his hatchet, Noel left his frow cleaving a log, and both came closer to hear.

"Looks like that'll be Lonesome Tilly all right," said Jonathan. "Deputy said he don't talk. As long as the old codger don't hurt nothin' . . ."

Willie burst out crying, his salty tears streaming down his face like a fresh.

"He'll hex you, Pappy!" he sobbed.

"Aw, apt as not, he's like a snake, Willie," offered Rob. "He won't hurt you unless you step on him."

The next morning, as the Venables stood about the clearing eating squirrel meat and the heron eggs Rob had found in a nest of sticks in a thicket near the river, Jonathan turned to Bertha. "I reckon the rock pickin' can wait till Noel can get at hit," he said. "Hit mought not be safe for young uns to get out of earshot till we figger out this Lonesome Tilly."

"There's plenty young uns can put their hands to closer home," Bertha assured him. "I 'lowed I'd take the clothes down to the river this mornin' and wash 'em. Steffy can help me, and Willie, you can watch Cassie and keep her out of the river."

It was hard for Stephanie to blot Lonesome Tilly out of her mind. As she stood knee-deep in the river, dousing Noel's faded linsey shirt in the water, she kept recollecting how like a scared little wild critter, a ground hog or a coon, he had padded away into the woods. All morning he stayed in her mind, dulling her pleasure in the sound of the ax as logs were notched and made ready to skid into place on the wall of the cabin. Were the Venable young uns likely to be running across him every time they went into the woods looking for huckleberries or chinquapins, chestnuts or possum grapes, she wondered. And suppose one of them, unbeknownst, crossed the old man, got his dander up? What would happen then?

When the sun was near the middle of the sky, Bertha sent Stephanie to the clearing to broil the pigeons Rob had snared in the woods that morning.

"You'd better run with her, Willie," Bertha said. "Cassie can play here on this big rock while I finish the washin'. I can keep an eye on her awhile."

Stephanie put Willie to gathering chips and dead twigs to lay on the coals of fire while she went to the spring for a piggin of water. No sooner had she dipped her piggin into the water, however, than she heard Willie shouting.

"Steffy!" he screamed. "Steffy! Come a-runnin'! The chickens have scratched up your seed!"

Water from the piggin sloshed on her skirt and drenched her bare feet as she ran up the hill toward the scene of the planting, but she was unmindful of her wet skirt slapping against her knees and clinging to her bare legs.

"Oh, Willie!" she scolded, tearfully, as she set down the piggin. "Why didn't you shoo 'em away?"

"I did," declared Willie. "When I saw 'em."

It was no time for complaining, Stephanie realized.

"Help me look for the seed, Willie," she commanded.

Side by side they squatted on the ground. Hawklike they studied the disturbed leaf mold while Stephanie raked her fingers lightly through it, back and forth, back and forth.

"Why didn't I bring more than one seed?" she moaned, as a film of tears curtained her eyes. "What ever possessed me? I could have brought a hundred just as well."

Suddenly she stopped her searching, wiped her eyes on the back of her hand, and looked at Willie grimly.

"Which chicken was doin' the scratchin'?" she asked.

"Josephine, I think," Willie told her, indicating the speckled hen which they had named Josephine because of her coat of many colors. "Anyway, she was stretchin' her neck and swallerin' when I looked," he added.

"Don't tell things you didn't see, Willie," warned Stephanie.

"I ain't tellin' things I didn't see," he said.

Stephanie studied Josephine a minute.

"Help me catch her, Willie!" she ordered.

"What you goin' to do with her?" he asked.

"Take that seed away from her," said Stephanie, grimly.

"How're you goin' to do a thing like that?"

"Don't ask questions," Stephanie blurted out at him, impatiently. "Just help catch her."

Ordinarily, catching the chickens was as simple as picking them up from underfoot. Now, however, Josephine, suspicious of their wariness, stopped her singing, dodged Stephanie's grasping arm, and ran for her life through the underbrush into the woods.

"Catch her, Willie! Catch her!" yelled Stephanie.

Away they tore through the underbrush, Stephanie scurrying around the hen to head her off, Willie guarding as well as he could all ways of escape to the rear. Step by step they hemmed her in until, at last, Stephanie grabbed her by the tail.

"Hold her!" she said to Willie, as she thrust the panicky chicken into his arms. "Sit down on the ground and hold her tight by the feet. And whatever you do, don't turn loose."

"What you goin' to do with her, Steffy?" asked Willie again.

Stephanie had no time to answer questions. Running into the woods, she borrowed Noel's hunting knife, then found among the household goods still heaped near the pine-bough pallets Bertha's steel needle, threaded with a coarse linen thread, lying in its small basket woven of grasses.

Hurrying back to Willie, she sat down beside him, turned Josephine upside down in his arms, and clenched her own hand over his small hand that held the hen's feet.

"Like that, Willie," she told him. "Make out you're a vise, and don't let her move a claw. Now, grab her around the neck with your other hand and hold her head back."

"I'll choke her," objected Willie, taking the hen gingerly by the neck.

"Don't choke her. Just hold her tight enough to let her know you will choke her if she gets sassy with you."

"What if she flogs me?"

"Let her flog! Anyway, only settin' hens flog. Josephine's too giddy to set and have a family."

Without more ado, Stephanie parted the feathers on Josephine's lumpy craw, gritted her teeth, slit the craw with Noel's knife, and emptied its contents into her skirt.

"Ugh!" squirmed Willie.

"Hold her!" warned Stephanie.

When she had satisfied herself by poking her finger about in the craw that nothing remained, Stephanie took the needle and neatly overstitched the slit.

"What if you kill her?" suggested Willie in an awed voice. "What'll Mammy say when she's dotin' so mightily on eggs? An' little bitty chickens?"

Over and over Stephanie stitched, a frown puckering her pointed face. Even when she finished, and cut the thread with Noel's knife, her blue eyes were clouded with fear of her own rashness. Gently she smoothed the feathers over the slit, and watched anxiously as she took the hen from Willie's hands and set her on her feet.

For a moment Josephine stood dazed—a long, anxious moment while she looked undecided as to whether she should live or die. Finally, she shook herself hard as if trying to wake up from a bad dream, and walked unconcernedly across the clearing.

"She sure is a tough old bird!" decided Willie, watching her.

Now that anxiety over Josephine had passed, Stephanie and Willie turned to the moist contents of the craw lying in Stephanie's lap. Bugs they found, dead and half-dead, and the seeds of grasses.

"There it is!" cried Willie. "See? That bug's got it!"

There, true as the gospel, was the seed of the Tree of Freedom, still satiny brown and none the worse for its misadventure, wrapped in the crumpled legs of a beetle.

"You can help me plant it again now, Willie," Stephanie said, "and this time I aim to pile brush on it so high that no thief on chicken's legs'll ever get in scratchin' distance of it."

Hardly had they covered the seed with leaf mold once more when out of the woods from the direction of Harrod's Fort came walking a stranger. Stephanie got to her feet, her heart pounding fast. He was not a buckskin, she noticed, such as a body might expect to meet up with in the wilderness, if he met anybody at all, nor a redskin, nor queer-looking like Tilly Balance. Nor did he look like a high-born Tidewater gentleman, though he wore the clothes of a gentleman—breeches buckled at the knees, low buckled shoes, long stockings, a long bright blue broadcloth shad-bellied coat, a satin waistcoat, a flowing cravat, and a low-crowned, broad-brimmed hat.

"Howdy!" said the stranger, as he came across the clearing. His voice was raspy, like the sound of a rat-tail file on metal. His dark face was deeply pock-marked, and his small, hard eyes bored straight ahead of him like gimlets.

"Howdy," muttered Stephanie.

"Run and fetch your pappy," ordered the man, jerking his head in the direction of the chopping. "I have business with him."

Stephanie hurried into the woods, Willie at her heels. At her summons, the Venables came traipsing into the clearing, Stephanie crowding close behind her pappy, Rob and Noel following with hatchet and frow, Cassie clinging to her mammy's hand, and Willie hanging on to her skirt.

"You Jonathan Venable?" rasped the stranger, eyeing Jonathan. "My name's Frohawk. Adam Frohawk."

"Howdy," said Jonathan, cold as an icicle. The other Venables strung out in a line beside Jonathan and stared at the outlandish stranger.

"I've got news for you, Venable," said Frohawk. As he spoke, he stuck his thumbs in his satin waistcoat pockets in such a way that a pearl-handled pistol came to light. "News you'll do mighty well to hear without stirring up any more trouble for yourself than you're already in."

"Spit hit out quick then," ordered Jonathan. Then he added, "This is the first time I knowed I was in any trouble."

"I'd say you're in plenty of trouble, noting all these improvements you're making about here, Venable," Frohawk said. "Happens that this land doesn't belong to you. Happens that this land belongs to a certain gentleman in the West Indies. Name of Garret Bedinger. Ever hear of him?"

"No more'n I ever heard of you," spat out Jonathan.

Noel shifted his weight from one foot to the other, and swallowed hard.

"Tell him to let you see his deed, Pappy," he said.

"Yeah, whar's your deed?" asked Jonathan. "Whar's your proof that anybody by the name of Bedinger 'way off at the end of nowhar has got any proper claim to this land? Let's see your proof."

Casually, Frohawk reached inside his big waistcoat pocket and took from it a silk wallet embroidered with threads of gold and silver. Out of the wallet he took a tattered piece of parchment, yellowed with age and much traveling about, and opened it up.

"Don't reckon anybody here can read," he said, "so I'll read it for you.

"By the King's Most Excellent Majesty and the Right Honorable the Lords of His Majesty's Privy Council:

"*Whereas,* Garret Bedinger, agent for His Majesty's Colony of Virginia, does, by his petition this day read at the

Board, humbly represent, that he being employed and instructed by the Government of that Country, petitions His Majesty for a confirmation of his privileges and properties under the great Seal of England; now,

"*Therefore,* upon full debate of the whole matter, it is ordered by His Majesty in Council, believing it to be for His Majesty's service that His loyal subjects should be settled on the aforementioned properties as speedily as may be, and anxious to repay such subjects generously for favors received, that the Right Honorable the Lord Chancellor do cause the said grant of 50,000 acres of transmontane lands lying in the neighborhood south of the Falls of the River Ohio, and westwardly to the Salt River, forthwith to pass under the great Seal of England accordingly.

"Signed, Philip Loyd.

"Fifty thousand acres," said Frohawk, hardly catching his breath after reading the parchment, "lying immediately south of the Falls, takes in this here little neckerchief claim of yours, Venable."

Stephanie glanced anxiously at her pappy. It didn't seem any more likely that he would have anything to say to these words inked in fine handwriting on a piece of parchment than he would have to say to the voice of God if it should speak to him out of thunder, or an earthquake, or a brightly burning bush.

Again Noel shifted his weight, and swallowed.

"Ask him, Pappy, has that paper got a date on it," he said.

"Yeah," echoed Jonathan, finding his tongue. "Has that paper got a date on hit?"

Adam Frohawk glanced at the parchment. " 'April 19, 1762. At a Court at Whitehall,' " he read.

"For once in my life I'd give my right hand, I reckon, if I could read writin'," sputtered Jonathan. "Then I'd know how much you're lyin'. Here," he added, suddenly pushing Noel forward, though it was as plain as day he grudged doing it, "let this young un see that paper."

"Certainly," agreed Frohawk. He smoothed out the parchment and held it close enough for Noel to read, but he was mighty particular to hold it out of his reach.

" 'By the King's Most Excellent Majesty, and the Right Honorable the Lords of His Majesty's Privy Council,' " read Noel.

Noel's voice in the stillness of the clearing was toned like a bell, and every word he read seemed to Stephanie to toll a death, as Bertha said the church bells of Charleston tolled when a body died. In this case, it was the death of this pleasant place overlooking a river where a cabin with a fine puncheon floor and a chimney of river rock was about to be raised, where a Tree of Freedom had been planted, and corn would soon be rustling in the hot summer winds. It was a tolling bell calling them to pack up their pots and pans, their flax hackles and Betty lamps, to load their creels on Job's back, to round up the cow, the sheep, and the pigs, and be on their way again.

"I only wanted to save you trouble, Venable," said Frohawk, as he folded the parchment when Noel finished reading.

"Whar's your pre-emption papers from the Land Commissioners?" asked Jonathan. "Whar's your surveyor's warrant?"

"Bedinger had the land surveyed years ago," Frohawk told him. "And pre-emption papers aren't necessary. Can't His Majesty grant such lands as he wishes to such subjects as he chooses?"

"Not this land," Noel shot at him. "Virginny does the grantin' in these parts now."

"All right. So Virginia does the granting in these parts," said Frohawk. "This deed's dated prior to October 26, 1763, and according to her own law, Virginia's bound to honor it. The Virginia Land Law says so expressly. It says that any person who has paid money into the public treasury under the regal government is entitled to receive vacant land. This upstart Virginia legislature took pains for good reasons to safeguard holders of old treasury rights. Too many Virginia bigwigs claiming Kentucky lands under such rights granted prior to October, 1763, to ignore that little matter."

"Whar's your proof this here Bedinger paid any money into the public treasury?" asked Jonathan, ignoring Frohawk's slurs. "Whar's your receipt showin' that?"

Frohawk opened up the parchment again, and read

like a slow rain that sinks into the ground as it falls, "'. . . and anxious to repay such subjects generously for favors received.'"

"Favors mought be money paid into the treasury, same as us honest, hard workin' folks pay," said Jonathan, "an' again, they moughtn't. They mought be spyin', or squeezin' taxes out of farmers, or stirrin' up the red men against us settlers. Any one of 'em, I calculate, 'd be a favor to His Majesty right now."

"That's quibbling, Venable," barked Frohawk, flatly.

Stephanie noticed Noel clenching his fists.

"You wait till Virginny gets her throat out of the stranglehold of His Majesty!" he blurted out, his gray eyes burning in his slim face. "Then let this Bedinger try to claim land he's done favors for! That's what Virginny's fightin' this war for now."

"Well! Well!" scoffed Frohawk. "One of the liberty boys!"

He turned back to Jonathan.

"You can move off now, Venable," he said, "and spend your energy on some other clearing you can hold on to, or you can go ahead here and lose everything you put into this patch of land. I take it you know the Land Law entirely. It provides, you know, that a court be held in December of this year when all contesting claims may be heard. Stay here, if you like, till then. Make as many improvements as you can. The more you make, the better it will be for Bedinger. But, if I were you, Venable, I wouldn't try to buck the law. It doesn't pay. Or," he added, looking straight at Noel, as he put the parchment back into his wallet, "His Majesty the King. Good morning, gentlemen. I'll see you again."

He turned on his polished heel and, like a raucous-voiced bird in fine sweeping plumage, he strutted across the clearing and disappeared into the woods in the direction of Harrod's Fort.

The Venables stared, first after Frohawk, then solemnly at one another. Jonathan slumped down on a stump and looked listlessly ahead of him, his shoulders wilting like an empty meal sack when folks are facing starvation.

Suddenly, however, he sat bolt upright, his eyes on the woods in the direction of the spring.

Quickly the other Venables turned about to follow his gaze, and stared awestruck as up the hill came Lonesome Tilly. A few steps he padded at a time, his scraggly white hair covering his stooped shoulders, his heifer-like eyes brimming with shy trust as he studied the curious faces before him. In his cupped hands he held a crude basket made of popple leaves pinned together with thorns.

Bertha Venable, after the first shock of seeing such a critter, took a step forward to meet him.

"You're Tilly Balance, ain't you, comin' to see folks?" she said.

It was a caution, thought Stephanie, how her mammy could smooth out a path for a stumbling body.

Shyly, Lonesome Tilly padded up to Bertha and held out to her the basket in which lay, heaped up and spilling over, sweet, red, wild strawberries.

"'Pon my word!" said Bertha, taking the basket from his outstretched hands. "And just when a body's starvin' for berries and such like! Here, Tilly," she motioned to a stump, "you sit right down here till we get dinner ready. It's 'way past dinner time, I reckon," she said, looking up at the sun which was already past the zenith, "but we got busy doin' other things."

Lonesome Tilly made no move to sit on the stump and wait for his dinner, however. He made no sign that he had understood a word Bertha had said to him. Instead, with a single grateful flash of his eyes toward Bertha, a look of recollection toward Stephanie, and a yearning in his face as he gazed a second at Willie, he slipped away among the trees as slick as a lizard.

"Well, consarn!" muttered Jonathan, ogling the spot where the old man had been standing so short a minute before. "If that don't beat the Tories! 'Quare old buzzard' is right!"

Bertha busied herself passing the basket of berries around for all to help themselves, and bit into the richly red, sweet-smelling meat of one herself.

"Quare or not, a good neighbor, I'd say," she

pronounced. "A mighty good neighbor. I've known lots worse."

"Did he put a hex on these berries, Mammy?" whimpered Willie, his mouth watering for a taste of them while fear kept him from reaching for one.

"Put a hex on 'em?" said Bertha. "Whatever put a notion like that in your head, child? Nobody can hex berries, honey."

She stood looking down tenderly at Willie, sensing he was not fully satisfied. "And can't anybody hex you but yourself," she added.

"Why don't he talk?" asked Willie.

"Maybe he was born that way," explained Bertha. "Or maybe it's a vow he took when somethin' or other happened to him away out yonder where he come from. Or maybe it's a sickness come over him out here in the wilderness by his lonesome with nobody to brew herbs for him, and gather slippery elm bark and lin bark and snake root to make him tea. It could have been a sickness that went to his head. Chances are, we'll never know. And I reckon we don't need to ask. We'll just take Lonesome Tilly as he comes."

"Will he come back?" asked Willie fearfully.

"I shouldn't be a bit surprised," said Bertha. "Now, stop frettin', and eat some berries."

She turned to Stephanie. "Whatever could you have

been doin', Steffy, all the time I thought you were startin' dinner?" she scolded.

"I—I got busy, too, doin' other things," Stephanie explained. "But I'll have the pigeons broilin' before you can say 'Wire brier,' Mammy. See if I don't. Here, Willie!" she called. "Where are the chips I told you to gather?"

7. Bad News from the Back Country

"I MOUGHT 'a' known somethin' like this'd happen," grumbled Jonathan as he finished his dinner of pigeon breast and strawberries. "Ever' day I been a-tellin' myself things were workin' out too fancy to be real. Now, 'long comes this feller Frohawk to tell me I'm right."

Bertha busied herself about the fire for a minute. "Nothin's happened, Jonathan," she said.

The clear, upstanding way she talked was almost enough to persuade a body to believe her.

"Nothin's happened, Jonathan. Just a little matter to prove you needn't go lookin' for trouble because it'll always find you. Run along, now, young uns. Noel, you and Rob get back to your choppin'. We've wasted a sight of time."

"But I couldn't for the life of me see how trouble such as this could find a feller 'way off out here in the wilderness mindin' his business," said Jonathan, taking little stock in Bertha's chipper dismissal of Frohawk's claims.

"Pappy," Noel spoke up quietly, "is what this man says about old royal claims such as Bedinger's right? Under the Virginny Land Law, I mean?"

"I don't know," said Jonathan. "I jist don't know. I jist took hit for granted that if a man had corn roots in the ground, an' a roof over his head, an' paid hard money for his land like the government said, that settled things. Didn't my own pre-emption papers set great store by the corn patch I planted back in seventy-eight?"

He shrugged his slumped shoulders and got to his feet.

"Nosiree," he said, "I never looked for trouble like this. Reckon we mought as well lay off work till I can go into the Fort an' get things straight at the Land Office. Reckon maybe the surveyor can tell me what the law is. Or the deputy. He knows ever'thing."

"If the law gives you till December, Jonathan," said

Bertha quietly, "I'd let the Land Office be, and finish this cabin."

"But what if that scoundrel—" began Jonathan.

"A lot can happen before December," Bertha told him. "The more improvements you have to do the talkin' for you in court, the less you'll have to use your tongue, and the likelier you are to win. A good cabin, and taters holed away in the tater hole, and shucky beans dryin' on the chimney, and corn for the hominy block—to my way of reasonin', no court's goin' to render a decision against such as these in favor of somebody that's never laid eyes on the land tryin' to hog such an eternal great big slice of Kentucky County. Honest work argues too loud. And besides, Jonathan," she added, "you can't buy up another claim. Your money's all gone."

"For all your reasonin', Berthy," Jonathan said, "justice ain't always on the side of common sense. An' that Land Office'll pay my money back or I'll know the reason why, if the court declares my claim ain't legal," he stormed. "They can take hit out of Bedinger's hide. Or Frohawk's."

"There's no use wastin' time in threats," Bertha reminded him. "Nor in talk. Nor in restin' ourselves. It's time to work, Jonathan. What work we do now'll talk mighty fine for us in December. Nothin's goin' to be decided, recollect, before December?"

It rubbed Jonathan against the grain to take Bertha's advice, but he went back to work. He had enough trees down, he reckoned, to build the walls of the cabin head high. As soon as he and Noel hacked out a path, he could wrap the log chain about the logs, hitch Job to them and snake them up to the clearing. It wouldn't take any time to skid them into place in the wall, he said. They were already stripped and notched. And when he got the walls raised and a makeshift roof on, he was quitting, he announced.

But if Bertha wanted a fine cabin before, she wanted an extra fine one now as if, once finished, it could stand up like quality folks and talk right back to Garret Bedinger and his agent Frohawk.

"Berthy, there ain't a lick of sense in havin' things so Frenchy, facin' what we face," complained Jonathan.

But Bertha had her way. The days, as they passed by, saw Noel smoothing floor puncheons with his broad ax and shaving them as smooth as a looking glass with his drawing knife so that barefoot young uns need not snag their feet on splinters; saw Jonathan make a trap door for the potato hole under the floor; saw him hew out a window and make a heavy wooden shutter, all to a grumbling tune. To a tune of louder grumbling they saw him build scaffolding for a bed in a corner of the cabin, and scaffolding for a table near the fireplace; saw Willie putting wooden handles on shells picked up along the river and whittling tines in sassafras wood so that the Venables might cat their vittles properly with spoons and forks; saw Jonathan and Rob and Noel roofing the cabin with the finest heart shakes of rived oak. They saw, too, sharp green quills of corn piercing the black loam in the clearing; saw beans unfurling their leaves like a Crusader's banner; saw the seed of the Tree of Freedom put forth a slender whip bearing downy, grayish-green leaves.

"I reckon, since we got ever'thing else finished to a Louis' taste, we mought as well build that fine rock chimney now," said Jonathan on the morning after the roof was pinned down with logs. "Noel, you an' Rob begin carryin' up the rocks from the river. Willie, you run help. Willie!" he shouted. "Wharabouts are you?"

At the sound of his voice, Willie came ripping from the woods on the east fringe of the clearing.

"Somebody's comin', Pappy," he blurted out. "From the Fort."

"Frohawk?" Stephanie asked him, trying to read the answer in his big, dancing eyes. "Is it Frohawk, Willie?"

"It's a man and a woman," panted Willie. "And some young uns. Leadin' a horse and drivin' a cow. Just like us."

The Venables didn't wait to hear more. They hurried around the corner of the cabin to see for themselves.

Through the trees from the direction of the Fort came, as Willie had claimed, a man, and a woman, and two small boys, the larger the size of Willie. The woman carried a sleeping baby in her arms, the man led a laden horse, and carried a rifle on his shoulder, while the larger of the boys drove a bony, brindled cow with a leaf-tipped switch.

Jonathan, followed by Bertha, hurried across the clearing to welcome them.

"Well, howdy, strangers!" said Jonathan.

"Howdy!" said the man.

The woman's face was a sight to see, one minute dark with wilderness worries, the next lighted up with relief till it looked as if she might be going to cry.

"You're Jonathan Venable, ain't you?" asked the man. "They told me at Harrod's Fort I'd find your place hereabouts. My name's Jason Pigot. My woman here, her name's Priscilla. Prissie, we call her."

"Come right in and sit down and rest yourself, Prissie," said Bertha, as she took the baby from the weary woman and led the way to the cabin. "I declare, if you ain't the very picture of a human bein' at the end of her rope!"

Prissie Pigot, however, couldn't drag her weary body into the fine new cabin. Instead, she sank down on the doorstep Noel had made of a short length of tree trunk, and rubbed her bare, scratched, swollen, aching feet.

"I begun to think we'd never make hit," she groaned. "Never in this world. The cow went dry an' we run clean out of anything to eat 'cept what we could find in the woods. For days now we been livin' like varmints."

"Well," soothed Bertha, "you got nothin' to do right

now but rest yourself. I count it a stroke of good luck you Pigots came along just when our cabin was in need of folks to help with a house warmin'. Here, Steffy," she said, laying the baby on the bed, "we'll pitch right in and get dinner. You run down to the spring, you and Willie, and look for poke sallet. Rob, you run right quick, you and Noel, and pop off some squirrels. This evenin' Jonathan can shoot some turkeys. And bring up some fresh water, Steffy. There's nothin' like cold spring water to put life back into a poor, gone body."

The day was a celebration for fair, with every Venable trying to outdo every other Venable in his welcome to the Pigots. Between traipsing off on errands for Bertha, Stephanie played with the Pigot baby, and picked up scraps of talk from Prissie and Jason.

The Pigots had come from North Carolina, on the Yadkin, she learned. Their claim lay across Salt River, on the western bank, and a little to the south of the Venables.

Yes, Jason had his pre-emption papers. He took them out of his shirt bosom and showed them to Jonathan, reeling off as he did so the bases for his claim—tomahawk rights, initials cut on a sugar maple tree near a sink hole, a shelter built. He couldn't read the writing on the paper, he said, but the deputy had seemed to think his was a rock-bottom claim. The deputy was coming out the next day, or the day after that, to survey the land. Until the claim was surveyed, the Pigots would stay with the Venables.

No, Jason hadn't heard a word of Garret Bedinger, nor of his agent, Adam Frohawk. Nobody had made mention of any such person claiming Salt River land.

The Pigots were like a crowbar for prying loose the tongues of the Venables and setting them to talking all at once. Though Jason Pigot was worn out with his long travels, he must examine every notch and corner, every shake and puncheon of the Venable cabin, and hear from Jonathan all the improvements he had made on his claim, and all he had in mind to make; how far into the woods he meant to girdle trees and extend his cleared fields that fall, how far the following spring.

"Leastways," Jonathan explained when he finished marking off for Jason Pigot the improvements he had in mind, "that's what I was a-goin' to do till this feller Frohawk showed up. Now I ain't so sure."

Willie showed the Pigot young uns where he had found the baby wood ducks, pointing the spot out to them from a safe distance as if he were afraid of surprising Lonesome Tilly again. And Bertha, Stephanie noticed, was full of the sort of talk to put backbone into a poor, dispirited woman like Prissie Pigot. Or maybe, thought Stephanie, glancing suspiciously at her mammy, Bertha was talking starch into her own backbone, so that she could face whatever December brought her.

Sometimes, for a moment, Stephanie forgot the cloud hovering over their claim as she listened to the talk about her. Something like singing was stirring within her. Now that neighbors had come, the spell of the lonely wilderness was gone forever. Back and forth, people would come and people would go. There would be cabin raisings for every family settling along the river. There would be corn huskings in the fall, and quilting bees in the winter. When enough people had settled around them, some Sunday a traveling preacher would hold a big camp meeting in the woods, and everybody for miles around would come to listen, and to out-sing all music, just as they did in the Back Country. And if her pappy felt too crowded, she reckoned a world filled with trees and bears and deer in which he could lose himself for a week at a time stretched a thousand miles beyond them.

That night after supper of turkey, speckled trout, and boiled wild duck had been eaten, and the least young uns put to bed on the pallets in the loft, Jonathan and Bertha, Jason and Prissie sat about the doorstep in the soft moonlight that drenched the clearing, talking, talking. Noel and Stephanie hung about on the edge, listening.

"Reckon you uns have heard the latest war news," Jason Pigot said. "Looked like Charleston was gettin' ready to fall when we pulled out. Lincoln, he ain't no general. Lets that British general, Clinton, cut a wide swath all around him. If Lincoln had a had an army 'stid of the two thousand raw militia he was able to muster, he mought 'a' fit hit out with Clinton. He claimed he was goin' to have ten thousand recruits, but hit was all big talk. They never showed up."

Down by the river a mockingbird in the top of a sycamore tree was spilling his wild song over the moonlit woods, and off somewhere on a grassy hillock a whippoorwill was whippering himself hoarse.

"Looks like nobody's had any stummick for fightin' since the British overrun Georgia as easy as back water at high tide. Even Marion's a-layin' low, they say, with nobody much a-joinin' up to help him."

A baby owl whimpered in a tree overhead, and on the river bank among the cane and the cat tails bullfrogs coughed and croaked a somber tune to go with the words Jason Pigot was saying.

"I used to think there was somethin' in this liberty stuff, mebbe," Jason went on, "an' no taxation 'thout representation, an' this here notion they call democracy. But looks like this here war's a-goin' to end one of these days. An' when hit does, His Majesty's goin' to be sittin' high an' mighty, as always, an' ever' single colony's goin' to be kowtowin' an' scrapin' an' bowin' around his throne an' claimin' hit was some other colony that started the fracas. They'll be a-harpin' on some other tune, I reckon, the colonies will, 'stid of that un folks have been singin' in the Back Country, 'The cause of Boston is the cause of all.' "

In the moonlight Stephanie noticed Noel's slim figure lean toward Jason.

"What's goin' to happen to the folks in Charleston if the British take it?" he asked. He was thinking about Uncle Lucien, Stephanie knew.

"Depends on who they are, I reckon," Jason said. "The militia'll be dismissed an' sent home, apt as not. That's the British pattern for handlin' the militia. The British know they don't fight wuth a continental. An' a body can't rightly blame 'em, I reckon. I wouldn't fight, either, if I was faced with a well-trained army havin' plenty of ammunition an' shoes on their feet an' vittles in their craws, if all I got out of fightin' was that no-account Philadelphy money. Or promises. Promises never fed a man yit. Nor put clothes on his back."

"What'll happen to the civilians?" prodded Noel.

"If they can prove they ain't never been disloyal to His Majesty in any shape, form, or fashion, they'll fare all right. I reckon the British won't be too hard on Tide-water folks, seein' as most of 'em are Tories, anyhow. Sympathizers with the British are turnin' up from be-hind ever' stump in Caroliny now. But if folks give any cause for suspicion, they'll be paroled. Put in jail, mebbe. Mebbe sent to Florida, or thrown off on one of the is-lands to die of fever an' shakes. Or smallpox. Smallpox is ragin' in Charleston now. Slaves brung hit in from Africy. Folks dyin' like flies. So many slaves a-dyin' of smallpox, they say folks jist won't bid any more on one that's never had smallpox. Hit's jist the same as throwin' his money away for a man to buy a slave 'thout pock marks on his face.

"Oh, I reckon all a feller's got to do to save his skin is to claim he's a loyalist," Jason said, getting back to the war. "He'll be all right. Of course, if he decides to be stubborn, like as not the British'll shoot him right in his own house an' turn his wife an' young uns out to forage in the woods. They've done hit many a time. That's why I reckoned now'd be as good a time as any to take to the wilderness an' let them as wants to fight hit out.

"Hit don't seem right," he added after a moment. "But what's a body to do when the country ain't got no sizable army, an' what hit has got is always wantin' to quit an' go home? An' look at hits generals. Look at General Washington. Still settin' there on his haunches eyein' Cornwallis as if that'd win a war. What's more, ever' colony from Massachusetts to Georgia is bankrupt, an' nine men out of ten'd be willin' to sell out to the enemy for a square meal, an' a promise that things'd settle down now an' folks could live peaceable. Folks are plumb wore out with this here war, and the country's in a mighty bad way, I tell you. Thanks to them fine speechmakers lawyerin' in Philadelphy."

Stephanie, though she tried hard to listen, heard little more that night. Long after she had gone to bed in the loft, she heard Jason Pigot's dark words set to the music of owls hoo-hoo-hooing softly in the woods, and the far-off screaming of a painter.

After a long time something on the other side of the loft moved. Stephanie turned her head. In the pale light cast by the moon through the undaubed cracks between the logs, she saw Noel get up from his pallet and peer outside.

She lay, stiff as a ramrod, watching and listening. Was he running away again? Was he going to try to cross the mountains and find the old Swamp Fox, Marion, and help him? Did he mean to try to find Uncle Lucien? And what would Jonathan say to all this?

Stephanie knew what her pappy would say. He would wake up as sure as shooting if Noel tried to get down the ladder and out of the door. He slept as lightly here in the wilderness as a hen with a flock of day-old chickens. And he would whip Noel as he had never whipped him before, with all the Pigots looking on. And Noel would go away inside himself, and this time he would lock the door. And nothing would ever be right. Nothing ever again.

She raised on her elbow.

"Noel!" she whispered sharply. "Go back to bed! Right away!"

Noel made no sign that he heard her. But in a minute he turned from the crack and lay down on his pallet again beside Rob. Stephanie lay awake far into the night until she heard him breathing deeply and quietly. Then she, too, slept.

8. Report from Charleston

THE ROOSTER awoke Stephanie the next morning as he rose on the limb where he had perched during the night, flapped his wings mightily, arched his long, gleaming neck, and hurled his screaming welcome to the sun.

Rising on her elbow, Stephanie peered across the cockloft to see in the dim light that Noel was still abed with Rob, Willie, and the two Pigot boys, and sleeping.

She lay back on her pallet, satisfied. But it was a short-lived satisfaction as the recollections of Jason's bad news from the Back Country and of Noel's actions in the dead of the night crowded in on her. Nothing seemed settled. Nothing seemed put in a place to stay, least of all, Noel.

It could be such a splendid day, she lay thinking, if only this thing she knew about Noel didn't keep stinging her like a sweat bee. As soon as the deputy showed up with his chains and his compass and tally pins, Jonathan would be going across the river with Jason Pigot to help survey the Pigot claim while the rest of the Pigots stayed at the cabin.

There wouldn't be a whole sight to make that day different from any other, Stephanie realized. The Venables couldn't have a company dinner such as Bertha would like to set before the Pigots, because company vittles would have to wait for the harvest. They would have their chores to do as usual—milking, calling up and counting the pigs which were growing sleek and fat, cooking, hoeing corn, beans, and potatoes, looking at the Tree of Freedom, hunting for double-yolked turkey eggs in rotten logs, and duck eggs along the river, helping Noel find the right piece of hickory for the rim of the spinning wheel he was making for Bertha.

But there would be cheerful noise around the clearing and in the cabin. Willie and Cassie would play the livelong day with the Pigot young uns, and the clearing would ring with their whooping and cutting up as they rode stick horses around the cabin, and played William-a-Trim-a-Toe and spat hand on the doorstep. And there would be talk to which Stephanie could listen all day long—little talk between her mammy and Prissie Pigot about things sure and familiar—about the baby's teething; about recipes for cooking bear's meat and potato pudding, apple fancy and gooseberry fool, punkin chips and wonders; about cures for the shakes and flux, rheumatism and snake bite; about shearing the sheep; about dyeing the yarn with onion skins, with shoemake and dogmachus, with a steeping of scrub-oak bark and maple bark, with pokeberry and alum, with the frail blue petals of the wild *fleur-de-Louis;* about spinning and carding and weaving.

For herself, Stephanie knew the day was going to hold no such trifling ease. She was going to stay within sight of Noel all day long, she promised herself as she buttoned her dress. If Noel had it in his head to run away again, she would help him, because she didn't want him caught a second time. It was a thing he had to do, she reckoned.

Noel yawned and opened his eyes.

"You'd better come and call the pigs, Noel," she said, as calm as a Sunday morning, "while I milk."

Stephanie, in all her imaginings, never expected Noel's chance to come as suddenly as it did. At breakfast, Bertha complained that their last grain of salt was gone and her duck egg without salt was as tasteless as cambric tea.

"You got salt, Jason?" asked Jonathan.

"Nary a grain," said Jason. "Salt like ever'thing else give out on the way over."

"Come fall, when the work ain't pushin' us so hard, we'll have to get together an' bile us down a supply," promised Jonathan.

"Reckon hit'd take a week hard runnin', wouldn't hit," asked Jason, "to bile down enough for both families?"

"All of that," Jonathan assured him. "Mebbe more. Jist depends. Hit'll take four to six hundred gallons of water for a bushel of salt, an' then hit can't hardly pass for salt, what with all the specks of dirt an' sech-like that manage to get biled up with hit. Noel," he added, "while I'm a-helpin' Jason with his surveyin' today, you mought go in to the Fort an' see if you can trade turkey eggs for some salt. Somebody mought have a little extry. Rob can go with you."

"I want to go with Noel, Pappy," spoke up Stephanie.

"No," said Rob, with his jaw set. "Pappy said for me to go. Didn't you, Pappy?"

"Don't make no particular difference," answered Jonathan, anxious to be off across the river and traipsing about Jason Pigot's claim.

"Then I'm goin'," decided Rob. "Besides, Steffy," he added, "Mammy needs you."

Rob's words were true enough, Stephanie knew. Between the hoeing and the grubbing, the cooking and the milking, the spinning and the dyeing and the weaving, Bertha had work lined up and waiting for her right down to Christmas. Today, however, Bertha would be too busy visiting with Prissie Pigot to ply her own hands overly much, or to recollect what Stephanie ought to be doing.

Stephanie felt panicky inside. Here was Noel's chance to run away being passed to him on a silver platter, the way Bertha said a slave passed meat on a silver platter to rich Tidewater folks, but if Noel wanted to reach out and take it, Rob would be nothing but a hindrance.

"Can't I go, Pappy?" Stephanie begged. "Just this once? In place of Rob?"

Jonathan looked down into her upturned face, and read the longing in her eyes.

"You let Steffy go this time, Rob," he said. "I 'spect the deputy could use a handy boy like you in the surveyin', same as he did before."

The sun was almost directly overhead when Noel and Stephanie, having gathered the big kettle full of turkey eggs, set out in the direction of Harrod's Fort. Noel walked ahead, his rifle on his shoulder, carrying the kettle, and in his shirt bosom a piece of jerk to stay their hunger. Stephanie again traipsed barefoot at his heels.

Changes, Stephanie noticed, had taken place in the woods since the day she and Noel went asking for the deed to the Venable land. The early blossoms had faded and gone. Now, in June, drifts of spoonwood blossoms, white and rosy pink, like the frail color of Tidewater seashells, swept down the hillsides waiting the touch of Stephanie's hand to spring and scatter a tiny shower of golden dust. Along the banks of the branch, wild blue *fleurs-de-Louis* grew with their roots in the mud, their blossoms with the air of France about them guarded by swordlike leaves; and on the touch-me-nots dipping in the stream tiny sweeplike buds were beginning to swell.

The earthy, springtime smell in the woods was gone, too. Now the woods smelled close and sickly sweet of the great, white waxen bowls opening on the cucumber trees, of the gaudy tulips blossoming on the yellow popple trees, and of the buckeye trees, each like a big green pyramid holding up a hundred pyramids of red. And on the bee trees, pale green blades were forming on the dark green leaves, sending forth slender stems on which tight buds were shaping.

Stephanie noted where the bee trees grew. In July a thousand starry blossoms would light the way for bees which, when they had sipped their fill, would likely swarm in the nearest hollow tree. She had little time that morning, however, to think of honey.

"Noel," she asked, as she plodded behind him through the woods, "do you reckon the British'll take Charleston?"

"Apt as not," said Noel, "if everything Jason Pigot tells is gospel."

"Supposin' they do," she said. "Do you reckon they'll behave the way Jason Pigot says?"

"Apt as not."

"What'll happen if they do?" she asked. "What'll they do to Uncle Lucien, do you reckon?"

"Put him in jail, apt as not," said Noel.

They trudged along silently for a distance.

"Seems like whatever happens to Uncle Lucien," Noel said, after a while, "I'll always carry him here inside me."

Stephanie wished she could look inside Noel's mind and see what thoughts lay hidden there. She found it hard to hack out a road to the thing she wanted to ask him.

"Noel," she finally blurted out, "you aim to go back to Caroliny and help Francis Marion, don't you?"

"Somebody has to help him," Noel said. "Else we're goin' to lose our chance. And then, apt as not, we'll never know what it's like to be a free people. We'll always wish we could have known, but we'll never know."

"If you want to go, Noel," Stephanie said after a moment, "if you want to strike out today while nobody's watchin', I think you ought to."

For a distance Noel trudged ahead, making no answer. Then, setting down his kettle of eggs and shifting his heavy rifle to his other shoulder, he turned and looked at Stephanie. It was a caution the pleasure that lighted his face.

"But it ain't that easy, Steffy," he told her. "A body can't do much by his lonesome. When I struck out the other time, I knew right where I'd find a nest of patriots I could fight alongside."

"Do you mean, Noel," she asked, feeling she had read none of his notions right, "do you mean you don't aim to go and fight?"

Noel smiled at the seriousness in her face.

"Of course, Steffy, I mean to go," he said, "when it's plain where I ought to go to. It's a long ways to Caroliny from here. It may be I'll be needed closer to home before us patriots win our chance to govern ourselves."

"Do you mean you think war's comin' to Kentucky?" she asked.

"It might," said Noel. "Or Kentucky might go to meet the war. As long as George Rogers Clark's loose, that can always happen. I'm just bidin' my time."

"When that time comes, Noel," she promised, "I'll help you get away."

Again they trudged silently, each understanding the other.

"My Tree of Freedom's growin' like somethin' possessed," Stephanie told him after a while.

"So I noticed," he said.

"I wish I could do somethin' for America," she confided, "like you're goin' to."

"Well, ain't you?" Noel asked. "Servin' your country's mostly honest work, Uncle Lucien says. And thinkin' ahead. You're doin' your share to found a new settlement in America, only you want to be on your guard like the de Monchards, not to make any deal with slavery of any sort. There's lots of slavery, Steffy, besides that you find in a black skin. And as for your chances, before His Majesty's redcoats quit plaguin' us, I 'spect you'll have plenty of chances to do somethin' for America. I aim to keep my ears open at the Fort today," he added. "May be able to run down some later news about Charleston than the Pigots brung."

There was no salt to be had at the Fort, they soon learned, but Noel traded the eggs for powder. A pack train of salt had been brought into the Fort a week ago, they were told, but not a grain of it was left. People were elbowing their way into Kentucky so fast, and all of them needing salt, somebody ought to open up a trading post and furnish salt to the settlers, folks said.

Talk of a trading post was only part of what Stephanie and Noel heard, however. Everywhere they went—to the spring for a drink of water, to the blockhouse to ask the surveyor if the preacher feller had been back to the Fort with his books, to William Poague's workshop to watch the fashioning of black gum ox yokes—they heard talk of Kentucky land. It was like a camp meeting song, thought Stephanie, the first line of which had been given out their first night in the Fort, grown louder with every verse.

Land was getting scarce, folks said. Oh, there was still plenty of mulatto land. But who wanted second-rate land? Supposing all the first-rate land was pre-empted. If a man had plenty of money, folks said, he could buy up land from holders of old treasury warrants and tomahawk claims by paying sky-high prices for it. Let land get out of the government's hands, and looked like it turned to gold in the twinkling of an eye. If a feller had land, they said, he ought to hang on to it by the skin of his teeth, for as sure as ever this infernal fracas with His Majesty was settled one way or another, land values in Kentucky'd go skyrocketin' higher than ever. And the smart folks'd be rich.

Once in a great while they caught snatches of a different kind of talk.

The way the British were stirring up the red men to raid Kentucky settlements didn't look a bit healthy, agreed the men talking in front of the schoolhouse. Especially between Harrod's Fort and the Falls on the Ohio, hardly a week went by without somebody getting scalped. Looked like the safest people in Kentucky were those who had built their cabins off in the woods by their lonesome, southwards of the Fort. The red men weren't fooling with them. They were scouting for big game and lots of it. Colonel Bowman had sent out spies to ferret out what the British and the Indians were up to, the men said, and the news the spies brought back didn't sound a bit good. The British might be trying to get even with George Rogers Clark for cooking their goose in the Illinois country, they said. Or they might be trying to draw off a lot of Virginia soldiers to defend Kentucky, so Cornwallis could make a quick killing of George Washington's army. It was hard to tell what was going on in their minds. But whichever way the British were figuring, it looked like trouble. Now if only Clark'd come back from the Illinois country . . .

Stephanie sharpened her ears at this talk of George Rogers Clark. No telling when Clark'd get back to Kentucky, said one man. Rumors were flying thick as milkweed seeds that the colonel had got him a dulce, the sister of the Spanish governor over in St. Louis. Love might make him hang overly long around the French settlements of Cahoky and Kaskasky and Fort St. Vincent.

Near the doorway of William Poague's workshop Noel and Stephanie came upon half a dozen men, one of them talking, the others nodding their heads as if what he said was gospel.

Looked like the war was petering out fast, mighty fast, the man said. He was a queer mixture of a man, noticed Stephanie, half Tidewater, half buckskin in his loose-fitting linsey shirt and his unkempt blue breeches buckled at the knee.

Every report out from the Continental Congress in Philadelphia looked gloomier than the one before, he norated. Back in January the Board of War had reported that, in spite of the fact the soldiers in the patriot army were half naked, it couldn't rig 'em out with any more clothes. Not even buckskins. Why? No money. Back in March the Commissary General of Issues announced there wasn't enough bread on hand nor anywhere in sight to feed the army ten days. Why? As usual, no money. And why should the Congress be reporting such gloomy news? Why didn't it set things right, collect the money for clothes and food instead of sitting there in Philadelphia strumming such a sorry tune? Looked like Congress was a sorry mess of stew.

And there was General Washington, said the man. It was hard to ferret out what was in the mind of Congress when they kept a man like Washington at the head of the army. A war was going on, to be sure, but General Washington wasn't fighting it. He hadn't fought a battle in two years. Looked like Washington's army was about washed up, he said.

The man would have said more, for he had got such a running start sledding the country downhill that it was hard for him to stop. At that minute, however, a man who was having a bridle mended in William Poague's workshop, ducked his head under the low doorsill and joined the group.

"You say the Board of War can't clothe the army, and

the Commissary General of Issues can't feed it?" he inquired.

The crowd fell back to make room for him. He was tall and dark, and his fine clothes that had the look of the Tidewater about them were wrinkled from long hours in a saddle. His manner, Stephanie noticed, was genteel and high-born to match his clothes, and as he talked, his keen black eyes bored through the bearer of bad news.

No, said he, the Commissary General of Issues couldn't feed the patriot army. There had been months when Washington's soldiers had scarcely tasted a vegetable, or salt, or vinegar, but it wasn't because there weren't vegetables and salt and vinegar to be had. It was because farmers and merchants from one end of the country to the other, all up and down the seaboard from Massachusetts to Georgia, could get more money and hard money by selling to the British. Traitor money, the man called it. Judas money. The selling of a dream as old as man for a bag of turnips.

And the Board of War couldn't clothe the army, either, the gentleman agreed. George Washington's army had never been outfitted properly. Sometimes Washington hadn't been able to march his men because too many of them hadn't enough rags to cover their nakedness.

And Washington, true enough, said the gentleman, when he wasn't just sitting still, was retreating. But if all General Washington had to do was fight the British, maybe he could get on with the war. Read some of Washington's letters to Congress, said he, and a body would have some notion of what the General was up against.

"Yeah," sneered the first man, "I've heard the gineral's good at writin' to Congress. But what the country needs is a gineral who can fight. The billydoos mought be left to somebody else."

"Maybe you know what General Washington complains about!" snapped the gentleman, his black eyes blazing clear back in their sockets. He looked exactly the way Noel was going to look some day when he found his tongue and could speak out what was inside him, thought Stephanie.

"Desertions, for one thing," said the gentleman. "As long as three years ago Washington warned Congress about desertions. Too many Europeans in his army—Germans and Irish and British. Every three out of four deserters that turned up in Philadelphia the winter Washington quartered at Valley Forge were born the other side of the Atlantic. Last year in the Eleventh Pennsylvania Regiment, the Old Countrymen outnumbered the American-born two to one. Why, half of all the regiment were born in Ireland!"

The first man tried to get in a word, but the gentleman gave him no chance.

"And who else is in Washington's army?" he flashed

out. "Loyalists. Prisoners of war. Convicts. Deserters from the enemy. Bounty jumpers. These are the men the states have sent to Washington. They're the men he's supposed to save the cause of freedom with. The rag-tag of the country. Give General Washington a decent-sized army of men who know the difference between freedom and tyranny, and who care, and he'd have Cornwallis whipped by morning. But he'll hardly get that kind of army when the rest of the country's interested more in getting its hands on money, and on black Kentucky land, than it is in freedom."

The man was like forked lightning, thought Stephanie, making everybody cower.

"The recruiting officers are not to be blamed for the sort of men they send General Washington, either," said the gentleman. "Naturally, the recruiting officers are hard put to it to supply an army when the citizens of a country can't see beyond their own tight, safe little world. It's not only Washington's army," he flashed out. "It's the American people—you, and I, and everybody else—that's about washed up. And that fine dream of freedom we had back in 1775 is about washed up with us. We may have health enough within ourselves to save our cause. I don't know. The chances are we'll have to have help from somewhere else. Maybe the French'll be good enough to loan it, though lately the French have talked out of both sides of their mouth. They're coming to help us, they say out of one side of their mouth. They're sending men, and ships, and hard money, they say. And out of the other side they're saying, maybe they'll make a separate peace with England. Any half-wit knows what a separate peace between France and England means—England with most of the seaboard bottled up and able to hold on to it. Spain claiming all the Mississippi country, right up to the Appalachians. That means Kentucky, too. Kentucky'll be under Spanish rule, if France makes a separate peace. And that nightmare, gentlemen—Kentucky under the flag of the Spanish gold diggers—is all too real since the British took Charleston."

Stephanie saw Noel's face go as white as the blossom on a bloodroot. His steel-gray eyes were fastened on the gentleman who stepped back into William Poague's shop with as little fuss as he had stepped out of it.

Quickly Noel followed him.

"Did you say—when did Charleston fall, Mister?" he faltered, standing in the doorway of the shop.

The gentleman, seeming to see Noel for the first time, fastened his black eyes on him like a burning light. Yes, he was the spit and image of Noel grown up, thought Stephanie, except for the color of his eyes and his hair.

"Charleston fell to the British on May twelfth, my boy," he said.

"Have you—any more news?" asked Noel.

"Not much that's good," said the man. "A fistful of patriots hiding out in the swamps and hills. They've a little ammunition, I hear, and pluck that's forged of iron. You know how they fight, maybe—hit and run, hit and run. It hardly seems possible that's going to defeat the well-fed, well-trained, well-equipped British army. But at present, it's the only thing we can do."

"Do you think—do you think American freedom is actually washed up, Mister?" asked Noel. "Like you said awhile ago?"

A slow smile lifted the veil of cloud off the man's face.

"Not, my boy," he said, "as long as you and I are alive."

Glancing at Stephanie, he added, "You and I, and your sister."

Outside the stockade Stephanie pressed close behind Noel.

"Who was that man, Noel?" she whispered.

"Pshaw! I didn't think to ask his name," said Noel. "It's queer, but seems like I know him mighty well, just the same."

Through the woods they hurried, saying little, scarcely noticing the squirrels that scampered overhead or the startled deer that high-tailed across their path, or the minnows that swirled in the branch, so wrapped were they in their own long thoughts.

Stephanie heard Willie's excited voice ranging the

woods in all directions as they came in sight of the clearing.

"Mammy, here comes the salt! Steffy, come and see what Lonesome Tilly brung me! Come and see! Hurry, quick!" he yelled.

"There wasn't any salt, Mammy," Noel told Bertha, but in the hubbub nobody seemed to remember salt as they followed Willie to a sapling at the edge of the clearing to which, by a whang of deerskin, was tied a baby raccoon.

"Lonesome Tilly brung it!" repeated Willie. "He brung it to me, my own self."

Stephanie squatted down and patted the little gray, scared mite, and ran her fingers gently along the black streaks that patterned its face.

"Did he say anything?" she asked.

"Nary a word," Willie told her. "Just brung this little coon to me, specially to me, and left."

"How'd you reckon he happened to know Willie wanted such a thing?" asked Bertha.

Stephanie looked down at Willie and smiled. "Just by lookin' at Willie, maybe," she said.

9. Express to Governor Jefferson

THE NEXT morning the Pigots got together their belongings, reloaded their horse, untethered their cow, and headed across the river to their claim. Jonathan put a bridle on Job and helped to set them across the stream, while the rest of the Venables looked on from the river bank.

Stephanie watched as Jonathan crossed the river for the last time, with one of the Pigot young uns riding in front of him, the other behind. She watched the Pigots line up on the far bank of the river in the order in which they had filed out of the woods into the Venable clearing so short a time ago—Jason in front, his rifle on his shoulder, leading his horse; Prissie next, carrying the baby in her arms, the smaller of the two Pigot boys at her heels, holding to her skirt; the older of the two behind, driving the cow with a leaf-tipped switch. Wasting no time, Jason headed into the woods, but Prissie turned for a last look across the river, raised her arm, and waved.

"Come over soon!" she shouted.

"You folks come back!" called Bertha.

Silently and swiftly the green leaves closed about them and they were gone, pushing the rim of Kentucky farther into the West, while the Venables climbed the hill to their clearing.

"I think I'll go to the Fort," Jonathan announced, as he led Job up to the clearing. "I aim to see if I can get wind of this Bedinger, or Frohawk, an' find out what they're up to. An' hit jist mought happen I'd run into a pack train of salt, Berthy. Noel, you'd better shear the sheep today, you an' Rob."

As soon as Jonathan disappeared in the direction of the Fort, Noel and Rob set about the shearing. Together they caught the sheep and lifted them, one at a time, to a short log that served as a shearing block.

Stephanie stood at the end of the block, her steadying hand on the overhanging head of the sheep. Though the critters panted from fright, and twitched when Noel raised welts on them or nicked so deeply with the shears that blood trickled out on their shorn hides, they never made a sound. They put Stephanie in mind of the verses Bertha read from her Bible about the Lamb of God.

Il l'interrogea donc par divers discours; mais Jésus ne lui répondit rien.

The washing of the wool fell to Stephanie. Taking Willie with her, she went down to the river and, tucking her long skirt above her knees, she waded out knee-deep into the water, dragging after her the creel in which the wool lay in long thick folds.

Up and down, back and forth, she swished and doused the creel, separating the matted wool to let the clear water run through it. Now and then she tore a cocklebur or an embedded stick-tight, a Spanish needle or a chain of beggar ticks from the strands. When at last the wool was clean and faintly yellow, Noel helped to carry it to the cabin, and spread it on the shakes to dry in the sun.

"Mammy," asked Rob as the young uns ate their vittles in the clearing at dinner time, "recollect what you promised me when we were crossin' the mountains? About the first shirt?"

"Yes," said Bertha. "I recollect. I've been wonderin'," she added, "who's goin' to get the second shirt."

"I am," piped up Willie. "I helped wash the wool."

"Reckon you could make out with the shirt you've got a while longer?" Bertha asked. "Or wear Rob's patched up old un when I make him a new un? If you could, I could make a shirt for a friend of yours."

"Who?" asked Willie.

"Your special friend who's always bringin' you things —berries and coons and such like," said Bertha.

"Lonesome Tilly? You mean Lonesome Tilly? Does he wear a shirt?"

"Do you think he grows fur on his hide, like a varmint?" asked Noel.

"Mammy," said Cassie, draining her noggin, "can I have some more milk?"

"Not till Steffy milks tonight, honey," Bertha told her, looking anxiously at her white face. "Looks like Brownie didn't give down her milk this mornin' like she ought."

Rob turned wide eyes on Bertha.

"Where is Brownie?" he asked. "I haven't seen her since we started the shearin'."

"I haven't seen her since I milked her this mornin'," said Stephanie, her eyes suddenly serious.

"She's down in the cane, mebbe," said Bertha, trying to cover her anxiety with casual words. "Noel, you'd better run look."

Stephanie followed Noel down the path to the river, both of them looking in every direction for some sign of the straying cow. But nowhere could they find hoof prints, nor trampled cane, nor signs of foraging among cane or leaves.

"What do you reckon's happened?" Stephanie asked,

her voice awed. It would have been what a body might expect if one of the pigs had strayed away in the woods and didn't come back. It was going to be a miracle if the pigs made out till hog-killing weather. All the Venables knew that. They had come to believe it with such certainty that they no longer whetted their appetites for backbone stewed in the big black kettle and covered with dumplings, for kidneys split lengthwise and broiled on a stick over the fire, and for thick slices of ham fried in the skillet.

But Brownie was a different matter. With her milk and her butter, she was to be their mainstay in the winter ahead.

"Noel," said Bertha, when he and Stephanie came up from the canebrake, "I was countin' on you workin' on my spinnin' wheel this evenin', but I reckon you'll have to lay off and hunt the cow. You'd better go with Noel, Steffy," she added. "And hurry, young uns."

As soon as Noel brought his rifle from the cabin, they set out in a northerly direction through the woods, where Rob had last seen the cow.

"Reckon we'd better hug the river," said Noel. "That way we can hunt through the cane and the woods at the same time."

Through the May apple bed where Lonesome Tilly had first been seen, they made their way. The hollow tree was now deserted, but the May apples, Stephanie noticed when she stooped and turned back some of the big green umbrellas, were beginning to turn faintly yellow. Farther on they found blackish sarvice berries clustering in a tree full of witches' brooms, and on the edge of an open, grassy spot a mulberry tree bearing little green August berries as hard as flint, and July berries as pink as a sunrise, and June berries as dark as a king's rich, royal purple.

When they had eaten their fill of the sweet purple berries, Noel studied once more the endless, still canebrake.

"Looks like we might as well leave the river," he said. "She couldn't have got into the cane without breakin' it down some place. Or at least, leavin' tracks."

After that, they kept to higher ground, going farther from the stream, and deeper into the woods. Every few paces they stopped and waited, searching in all directions, and naming to each other the sounds they heard. Squirrels scampered and scolded overhead and chattering blue jays flashed their wings among the green leaves. Overhead, out of sight beyond the bushy tree crowns, crows cawed, and now and then a chipmunk scampered among the fallen leaves, or a grayish-green lizard slithered up the butt of a tree. But nowhere was there a sign of a straying cow.

"Hadn't we better turn back?" Stephanie asked at last, noticing how slanting were the sun's rays that broke now and then through the trees.

Noel stood a minute, considering.

"She'll be farther away by mornin' than she is now, I reckon," he said. "We'll go a hill and a holler farther."

Again they trudged ahead, silently, across a small ravine, as fronds of maidenhair fern whipped softly against their ankles.

They stopped on the brow of a hill. Noel lifted his rifle from his shoulder and let the long barrel slide through his fingers till the butt rested on the ground. He stood motionless, his eyes peering through the woods. Stephanie stood beside him, her face warm and flushed.

"We'd better go back now, Noel," she whispered. "Before dark overtakes us."

Noel, however, made no move to go. He continued to stand and listen, sorting out the woodsy sounds all about them, the occasional scurry of padded feet, the questioning chirp of birds, the faint movement of leaves in the still afternoon.

Suddenly Stephanie touched his arm.

"Listen!" she whispered.

"I don't hear anything," Noel told her after a minute.

Stephanie cocked her head toward the river.

"Pipin'!" she said. "Somebody pipin' a tune on a reed. And look!"

She gripped Noel's arm tightly as she pointed into the woods ahead of them. Her face was blanched with fear.

"Somethin' moved down there in that lin tree," she whispered.

Noel tensed. Raising his rifle, he stood ready to fire.

"It jerked like somethin' jumped in it," Stephanie whispered. "Or out of it. Reckon it was a bear?"

Noel studied the tree, his fingers on the trigger of his rifle.

"Bears don't show any likin' for lin trees, I reckon," he said.

As they watched, the branches on the farther side of the lin tree bent a little, dipped low, then swung free again.

"It's just a deer," whispered Noel. "Didn't you see an ear a-twitchin'? I might shoot it and skin it, and we could carry home some of it. Mammy'd like a mess of venison, I reckon. And I could make us some moccasins out of the hide."

He took aim with his rifle and squinted down the long barrel.

"Don't shoot, Noel!" begged Stephanie.

There was no telling what the loud noise of a rifle might scare up in the woods, she told herself.

"Let's keep a-watchin'," she begged, "till we're sure."

As they watched, the branches bent again, dipped, and swung free, and again Noel aimed at the spot where a furry ear twitched.

With a panicky feeling tearing at her, Stephanie

watched him, dreading the sound of the rifle. What had got the matter with her, she wondered. Had the stillness and the dimness of the woods demented her that she couldn't bear to hear a rifle shot when it meant thick broiled venison for supper, and a pair of new moccasins to wear whenever she went to the Fort?

Noel lifted his fingers from the trigger and spat on them.

A low, familiar "Moo-oo-oo!" greeted him, and through the branches of the lin tree, Brownie thrust her long, brindled head.

"Consarn!" muttered Noel. "What if I'd shot her?"

The thought of such a disaster sent a shiver down his back.

"How did that critter ever get way over here at the end of nowhere 'thout leavin' any trace?" he wanted to know as he shouldered his rifle.

"She must have gone through the woods another direction," Stephanie told him.

"Well, why did she have to traipse over here when there are plenty of lin trees close home?" Noel demanded. "She's got itchy feet, I reckon. Come on, Brownie!" he called, holding out his hand as he walked down the hill toward her. "Sooky! Sook! Sook!"

He had almost reached the cow when Stephanie called him.

"Listen, now, Noel!" she said, softly. "Down by the river. Don't you hear it?"

Faintly through the trees came the sound. On a willow reed somebody was piping a shrill tune, though to be sure it seemed to Stephanie to be no such tune as Noel sang to accompany the ballads he played on the dulcimer, or the songs sung at the Presbyterian camp meeting. The notes seemed to wander up and down, going high or going low, as fancy struck them, like some playful woodsy critter feeling good in the sun.

Noel climbed the hill again and stood beside Stephanie. They listened a minute longer to the aimless fluting that spattered the woods with clear, sweet sound.

"Let's go and find it," suggested Noel.

"Oh, but it might be red men," Stephanie told him.

"Red men don't pipe like that," said Noel. "Red men don't pipe at all. Listen! That music ain't got killin' on its mind. Can't you tell?"

He started slowly in the direction of the music. Stephanie followed him skittishly.

"What'll we do with Brownie?" she asked.

"She won't stray now," said Noel. "Anyway, we won't go far. And we'll come right back and get her."

Stealthily they made their way along the slope, stopping every few paces to listen as the piping grew clearer. Following the sound put Stephanie in mind of Back Country tales she had heard of young uns being lured into danger by listening to mortal sweet music. She wanted to turn back, but Noel was for going on. It was a caution, she thought, how Noel took no stock in witches and ghosts and ha'nts, in lights gleaming on water, and roosters crowing at the front door, and death bells ringing.

On they went, one stealthy step after another, and closer and closer grew the fluting.

Suddenly Noel stopped. As quietly as a stalking red man, he parted the underbrush and motioned Stephanie to peep through. So close to them that they were almost on the banks of it, a little flag-fringed branch rippled down toward the river, and in its elbow rested an open place, green with grass and gold with evening sun. On the edge of it, with his bare legs crossed under him, sat Lonesome Tilly, playing on a willow reed. A blue dragonfly with gauzy outspread wings fluttered about his knee, dipping and rising, dipping and rising and dipping. But whether the dragonfly was dancing to Tilly's piping, or Tilly was piping to the dragonfly's dancing, a body couldn't tell.

"I wish I could see what that old man's a-thinkin'," Noel whispered.

A dead twig snapped underneath Stephanie's foot, and quick as thought, Noel let go of the underbrush so that the limbs sprang back and hid them.

But the noise put an end to the piping. After staring for a minute at the bushes, Lonesome Tilly got up, slipped his pipe underneath a wide whang tied about his waist, and disappeared behind the bearskin that served as a door to his tiny cabin built against the side of a hill.

"Shucks!" muttered Noel. "He's awful easy scared. Let's go see him."

But Stephanie pulled at Noel's arm. "We got nothin' to take him," she said. "Not even mulberries. And we hadn't ought to go without somethin' because he always brings somethin' to us. 'Twouldn't be like neighbors to go empty-handed."

Noel took a last look through the bushes, but Lonesome Tilly did not come again from behind the bearskin.

"Leastways," said Noel, "we know now where he lives. We can come back some time and bring him somethin'. Maybe the shirt Mammy's a-goin' to make for him."

It was owl light and supper was ready when finally they reached their own clearing, driving Brownie before them. They had hardly finished telling Bertha about Lonesome Tilly and the music he made on his willow reed when Jonathan came home from Harrod's Fort.

"Did you get any salt?" Bertha asked him.

"Naw. No salt," he said. "Some in a week or two, mebbe."

"Did you see Frohawk?" asked the young uns.

"Naw. Didn't see Frohawk. Seen another feller."

"Who, Pappy?"

Jonathan didn't answer. He ate his supper silently, as if he hadn't heard their question.

When Willie and Cassie were sound asleep in the cockloft, Jonathan called the other Venables into the cabin and bolted the door.

"Seen Colonel Bowman at the Fort," Jonathan told them, his voice low, like a bur in his throat. "He wanted me to do a little job for him."

By the faint light of a Betty lamp, Jonathan took from his shirt a piece of paper no bigger than his hand, with writing scrawled on it. He cleared his throat, making ready to tell them what the paper said, when Bertha got in the first word.

"Didn't you hear anything at the Land Office about Frohawk, Jonathan?" she asked.

"Couldn't find a soul that knowed anything for sure," said Jonathan. "Surveyor said he ain't had no notice about any sech claim as Bedinger's, but one could still turn up, he said. That's all I could get out of him."

He cleared his throat again. "From all I could pick up 'bout the Land Law," he said, "seems like Frohawk mought be able to claim this land when the court opens. Don't look worrit, now, Berthy, 'cause for ever' down in life, there's an up."

It seemed to Stephanie that her pappy was singing a spryer tune than usual. Ordinarily he didn't argue so cheerful-like.

"Under that part of the Land Law that says them as possess old treasury warrants to the land dated prior to 1763 has a legal claim to hit," continued Jonathan, "this Frohawk could make trouble. That's what the surveyor said. An' jist as I was makin' up my mind to fight hit out in court, why 'long comes Colonel Bowman with this job for me which was the same as sayin', let Frohawk claim this land if he can, there's a thousand acres of better a-waitin' for the Venables."

Bertha eyed him sharply. "You don't make good sense, Jonathan," she told him.

"Here, Noel, read this here," said Jonathan, handing him the paper.

Noel took the paper, faced it toward the flickering light, and read:

"The bearer, Jonathan Venable, is sent express to the Governor upon business of the utmost consequence to the State. Justices of the Peace in the several counties through which he may pass are requested to aid him in his journey with fresh horses, information, &. &. Colo. John Bowman,

Lieutenant of Kentucky County."

"That little scrap of paper's wuth four hundred dollars, hard money," said Jonathan with a mighty satisfied look on his face, as he took the paper from Noel and stuffed it into his shirt bosom again. "An' four hundred dollars'll pay for one thousand acres of land, finer even than this. Over on the Green River, they're openin' up land, I hear. Course, I had to bargain for hit right sharply," he added. "Afore I'd sign up with the Colonel, I went about askin' how much an express gets paid nowadays for carryin' important messages. Two hundred dollars for short trips, they said; as much as three hundred fifty to four hundred for long trips. The red men an' the

British eggin' 'em on from behind are what makes expressin' come high nowadays. But I says to myself when the Colonel an' me come to terms, I'm a-goin' to fight this here Frohawk's claim tooth an' toenail. But if I have to lose, hit can't ruin me."

"What's your business with Governor Jefferson?" Bertha asked, staring at Jonathan with eyes full of questions.

"I'm swore to secrecy," said Jonathan. "Even from my wife an' young uns. I carry my business in here," he added, tapping his forehead, "where Colonel Bowman hisself put hit."

"When are you leavin'?" Bertha asked.

"Sunup," said Jonathan. "Not a minute to lose."

"Maybe the Indians'll come here while you're gone, Pappy," suggested Rob.

" 'Tain't likely," Jonathan said. " 'Tain't likely they'll cross the Ohio in any strength. Leastways, not if George Rogers Clark gets back from the Illinois country. The air Clark's a-breathin' is mighty onhealthy for the red men or the British, I reckon, an' they know hit. If anything happens, I got a boy at the Fort promised to run out here an' warn you. Then you're to move in, Berthy. D'you hear? An' Noel," he hurried on, not waiting for Bertha to answer. "You're to be the menfolks around here while I'm gone. You an' Rob go tomorrow an' help Jason Pigot with his cabin. Then go right along tendin' the corn an' clearin' land like you never heard tell of Adam Frohawk, like you aimed to stay here the rest of your borned days. An' if that old geezer turns up, no matter what shape he comes in, take care of him. Don't take no sass off him. No sass at all."

Noel sat there, looking white around the gills. Stephanie suspected he was hearing his pappy with one ear, and Francis Marion and his fistful of patriots with the other. And of the two, she thought he could hear Marion a shade clearer.

"Noel," Jonathan spoke up sharply, "did you hear me?"

"Yes, Pappy, I heard you," said Noel.

"You ain't actin' exactly like hit," said Jonathan. "Berthy, I ain't heard you promise to fort in case of red men."

"Don't seem to me there's an awful sight of choice between bein' scalped quick by a tomahawk," she said, "and takin' three weeks to die slow of starvation such as I know there'd be when two or three hundred get behind them stockades with not a mouthful to eat. We'll look out for ourselves, I reckon, Jonathan. And if we have to fort, we will."

Jonathan studied them a minute silently. "Reckon mebbe you boys'd better not go to help Jason Pigot tomorrow," he said. "While I'm gone you'd better stay close home. The Pigots can live in a half-faced cabin for a spell. I'll help Jason when I get back."

Stephanie climbed the ladder to the cockloft that night with a strange feeling of fear of red men. To be sure, red men hadn't bothered settlers to speak of since George Rogers Clark set foot on Kentucky soil. Let a body whisper Colonel Clark's name to the red men, and right away, as if it were a plague of murrain pronounced on them, they hotfooted it back across the Ohio. But Clark wasn't in Kentucky now, she reminded herself. He was over in St. Louis where he had a Spanish dulce. Maybe the Indians knew that. Maybe that was why they were thickening in Kentucky again.

But a body had to hold on to her fears, she told herself. A body had to shut her fears up tight inside herself, and let nobody see them, least of all, her mammy.

10. A Soldier for Colonel Clark

MORE than once, as Stephanie milked Brownie the next morning, her eyes strayed in the direction Jonathan had taken to Harrod's Fort on the first leg of his journey to Williamsburg, as if she were trying to ferret out the mysterious errand on which he had been sent. Could the gentleman she and Noel had seen at William Poague's workshop have had something to do with the message? she wondered. But the silent dark wall of trees kept as secret as a bury hole her pappy's whereabouts, and his doings, and all that befell him.

Mid-morning Rob fell to speculating on the length of time it would take his pappy to make the trip to Williamsburg and back again. A horse could jog along steadily at the rate of five miles an hour, he calculated. At that rate, if Jonathan rode ten hours a day, he could cover fifty miles between sunup and owl light. But Colonel Bowman had mentioned fresh horses. That meant he expected Jonathan to spur his horse along at a gallop wherever he found a road.

"Jeeminy, criminy, what kind of message do you reckon Pappy's a-carryin' to the Governor?" asked Rob, when he got this far in his calculations. "The Colonel's sure in an all-fired hurry if Pappy has to run a horse all the way to Williamsburg."

"The Colonel's had spies out," Noel told him. "He knows things."

Rob looked at him sharply. "Are the Indians comin'?" he asked.

"Not as I know of," Noel told him. "But somethin's goin' on, you can be sure of that, when it costs so much to send an express to the Governor, and Colonel Bowman's willin' to pay it. A body's reason'd tell him that much."

After a minute Rob went back to his calculations, but it wasn't long before he broke plumb down in them, not knowing how far it was to Williamsburg, nor how fast Jonathan would travel, nor how long he'd have to parley with the Governor once he got there.

"You'd have more to show for your time grubbin' bushes and choppin' nettles and water weeds out of the corn," Bertha told him, and sent him, grubbing hoe in hand, to the corn patch.

Stephanie had never seen corn grow so fast as theirs. Sometimes she stood and eyed a stalk, trying to catch it in the act of growing. Before long prop roots would be putting out at the bottom of the stalks to hold the corn steady during the ripening, stiff tassels would shoot out of the top, and batches of waxy, dark red silks would spill out of the middle. It was the black Kentucky land that made the corn grow like something possessed, said Noel. It was little wonder, he said, men lost their reason trying to buy it up.

Grow as fast as the corn would, however, it couldn't grow fast enough to satisfy the Venables. Every day the young uns named what they would give for just one slice of hoecake, until Bertha, watching their pinched faces, made up a game for them. The juicy white breast meat of the turkeys Noel shot, they could call that bread, Bertha said. The fat, heavy flesh of bear, and the strong, dark flesh of the buffalo, that was meat, she said. It was a good game, agreed the young uns, but it left them as hollow as the Joe Pye weeds through which they blew bubbles down by the spring.

The Tree of Freedom grew, too. It didn't grow as fast as the corn, nor as gangling as the pumpkin vines that sprawled among the corn. It didn't grow as fast as the potatoes on which clusters of white blossoms would soon be opening up, nor the gourd vine on which every day the young uns looked to see if little bitty long-necked gourds were beginning to set. The Tree of Freedom, having half a hundred summers instead of one in which to grow, took its time.

"Steffy," said Willie one day as he watched her tend the tree, "whoever heard of hoein' a tree to keep it alive when some day ever' endurin' tree in the woods is goin' to be girdled to make room for corn? A body'd think you was that tree's mammy, the way you baby it."

"Maybe I am," she said.

The days were long now, but there was never time to be idle. A body'd think Bertha felt winter breathing down icy breath on them in the midst of summer heat, the way she had all the young uns scurrying around. Or maybe, thought Stephanie, work was her mammy's way of hanging on to her reason, with Jonathan gone, and red men off in the woods some place, with winter coming, and a passel of mouths to feed.

First, they had to build the chimney. For three days they lugged rocks up the hill from the river—big rocks and little rocks which Noel chipped and smoothed and fitted into a wall around the wide space left for them at the west end of the cabin.

When the chimney was finished, Willie and Cassie ran in and out of the big fireplace, and turned their faces up and hollered into the wide, yawning funnel. Bertha got together all her tools and utensils she had brought from the Back Country—her pothooks and trammels, her kettles and her skillet, her griddle and her trivet—and carried them to the hearth.

"Now," sighed Stephanie, as she saw the kettles on their pothooks swinging from the crane Noel had fastened in a side wall of the fireplace, "it's home at last!"

Rob sighed, too, but for another reason. "It'll sure take an eternal great big back log to fill that fireplace," he said. "Did you need to build it so big, Noel?"

Bertha wanted a spring house built about the spring, too. Again the Venables lugged rocks from the river, while Noel laid three walls, leaving the fourth side open. Halfway up the walls, he fashioned a ledge by recessing the upper walls, which he built of smaller stones. Here on the ledge Bertha could set her wooden bowls of butter, while piggins of milk could stand in the running water of the spring to keep cool and fresh and sweet. Noel cut bars of saplings to lay across the front to keep varmints out, and laid a roof of bark on a skeleton of saplings.

The stump of a sycamore standing near the cabin would be mighty handy for a hominy block, Bertha decided. By burning and chipping and scraping, Noel gouged a hole in the stump big enough to hold a kettle full of corn. Then he cut a long sapling for a sweep and wedged the butt end of it under the bottom log of the cabin. A shorter sapling, trimmed just above the forks, he drove into the ground between the cabin and the hominy block, and rested the sweep in the crotch. To the free end of the sweep he tied another piece of sapling, one end of which he had chipped round to make a pounder.

"Try it out, Rob," he said, when he finished it.

Rob grasped the pestle in his hands, and putting his weight on it, drove it down into the hollow stump, then let the wedged sweep lift it. Half a dozen times he pounded the block with the pestle, then stood off and eyed it longingly.

"If a body just had a little corn in there!" he sighed.

As soon as Noel finished the hominy block, Bertha set him to work on an ash hopper. Stephanie held the shakes in place for him as he built the hopper in the shape of a V, letting the bottom of one row of shakes extend a little below the other row to allow the water poured over the ashes to trickle down and drip into the kettle Bertha would place underneath.

"Looks like a body'll never get within hailin' distance of all Mammy wants done," Rob complained to Stephanie as he went to the woods to look for a wild cherry tree from which to make a butter paddle. "I'll bet there ain't another clearin' in Kentucky with so much work laid out for young uns to do."

Their clearing was a busy world, to be sure, thought Stephanie, but such a lonesome, tight little world, hemmed in by trees. Not a soul came near it, not even the Pigots, now that they were busy in their own clearing. And not a jot nor tittle of news filtered to them through the woods. Nor did Jonathan come home.

"Apt as not, the Governor's sent him somewheres else with a message," Bertha told the young uns, to keep long faces off them when it began to get dark.

"Do you reckon the red men have scalped Pappy?" asked Willie, not knowing he oughtn't to say such words.

"That ain't likely," said Bertha. "The red men ain't so smart they can scalp a body with his wits about him." After a time she added, "Nothin' that sneaks'll get you if you're waitin' for it when it comes."

When June had passed its prime, Bertha said again at dinner one day that she didn't think she could stand another bite of vittles without salt.

"Noel, you and Steffy try at the Fort once more," she said. "Take a kettle full of sarvice berries and maybe somebody'll trade you salt for 'em."

But Stephanie knew that more than salt her mammy was hungry for some scrap of news of Jonathan.

As soon as they had gathered the sarvice berries, Noel and Stephanie set out. Almost a month had passed since they had gone that way in hope of salt the first time. Now the woods were dark and glistening green, and noisy, not with birds, but with harvest flies whizzing their timbrels among the trees, and locusts drumming among the grass blades in the open spots, cutting so deeply with their noise that they left a scar on the memory. Snakes slithered across the path, and along the edge of the branch darted sleek, blue-winged dragonflies like the dragonfly for which Lonesome Tilly fluted on his willow pipe.

Within half a mile of the Fort, they stopped to rest at the foot of a hill. Noel squatted down and squinted his eye over a crawdad hole.

"Can you see him?" asked Stephanie.

"No," said Noel, "but I think I hear him."

Again he squinted into the hole.

Suddenly he cocked his head, his gray eyes alert, and strained his ears to listen. Not being satisfied, he laid his ear flat to the ground.

Stephanie, watching him, gathered up her long skirt.

"What d'you hear, Noel?" she whispered.

Quicker than a wary varmint of the woods, Noel was on his feet.

"Better hide, Steffy!" he ordered. "Somebody's comin'!"

Off the path they darted. As flat as lizards they sprawled behind a fallen tree screened from the path by bushes. Noel trained his rifle on the path.

A minute passed while Stephanie's heart pounded underneath her cottonade dress. Then they could hear, and no mistake about it, the soft thud of feet on a path that skirted the hill from the east. Many feet, it seemed, were running on the springy leaf mold.

Stephanie crouched closer to Noel.

"Sounds like some of the feet are fastened to young uns," Noel whispered. "Hear?"

Stephanie listened. Quick, heavy footsteps she heard, and, true enough, double quick little ones.

A moment later, along the path came hurrying a man with a rifle on his shoulder and a big bundle tied in a deerskin on his back, a woman carrying a baby in her arms and a young un on her back, while two little scared young uns holding tight to her skirt trotted behind her.

Stephanie raised her head high over the tree trunk to stare at them.

"Fortin'!" she said, her eyes wide. "Wonder why?"

"There ain't but one reason why folks fort," Noel said, giving words to her fears. "We'd better find out where the red men are."

He got to his feet and walked stealthily toward the path.

"Reckon it'd be best to play safe so as not to get shot," he mumbled, taking a stand behind a tree. "Hello!" he shouted.

The man dropped his deerskin bundle, whipped about, and readied his rifle in the direction of Noel's voice. The woman, looking like a trapped deer, tried to run, but she was too hobbled with whimpering young uns to make headway.

"Who air ye?" quavered the man.

"White folks and friends," called Noel.

The man waited a minute. They could see him

through the bushes, taking aim in their direction, wetting his lips.

"Show yourselves!" he ordered.

Out of the bushes stepped Noel and Stephanie to assure the strangers, then hurried to meet them.

"Be ye comin' to the Fort?" asked the man, breathlessly.

"Yes," Noel told him. "Has somethin' happened?"

"Happened? Hain't ye heard?"

The man stared at Noel, his eyes a whirlpool of dark fear in his strained face.

"Boy, where ye been? Didn't nobody warn ye? The red men done finished Ruddell's an' Martin's over on Lickin'. Hundreds of 'em come pourin' over the Ohio. This mornin'. Hauled up a British cannon, an' them stations was a gone Josie!"

Goose bumps popped out on Stephanie's arms. She crowded closer to Noel.

"Whar do you young uns live?" asked the man.

"Over on Salt River," said Noel. "West of here a ways."

"Didn't no runner come an' warn ye?"

"No. Nobody came. We didn't know anything about the red men."

"Course, the red men air over yonder t'other direction from you," the man said, thoughtfully. "They ain't been over your way."

"Well, 'tain't no time to mouth 'bout it," whimpered the woman. "Let's get to the Fort."

"I could go back, Steffy, and see if Mammy's safe," considered Noel. "But maybe we'd best go to the Fort since we're so close, and get things straight. 'Twon't take me no time to run home by my lonesome when we hear all the news."

The Fort was a sink hole of hubbub and hurry and fear that sucked Noel and Stephanie into it as soon as they set foot inside the stockade. From all directions panicky families came squeezing in, the grown folks carrying whatever they could grab up in a hurry—a rifle, a knife or two, an ax, a few clothes tied in an old coverlet, some jerk to stave off hunger if the Fort should have to last out a siege, a piggin, sometimes pieces of pewter, a few spoons, a plate, a candlestick. Some of them drove cows into the Fort, hurrying the poor, bewildered critters along with the sting of a willow switch. A few young uns, Stephanie noticed, came clutching a kettle or half a dozen pewter spoons or whatever had been hurriedly thrust into their hands. One little girl the size of Cassie hugged a rag doll to herself, and a little boy squeezed a kitten in his arms. All of them were shooshed teetotally into being quiet as they were dragged from their clearings through the woods to the Fort.

Rumors flew about the stockade like miller moths darting around a lighted Betty lamp. The men at Ruddell's and Martin's had all been killed. No, the men hadn't been killed, only the women and the young uns. No, the women and the young uns were taken to Detroit.

No, the young uns were scalped alongside the men, and only the womenfolks were taken to Detroit. The red men had left Kentucky. The red men, egged on by General Bird, the British commander, were still in Kentucky, headed straight for Harrod's Fort, bringing their cannon with them, burning and looting and scalping as they came. No, the Indians had all got drunk after taking Ruddell's and Martin's, and General Bird couldn't persuade them to march on Harrod's Fort. He had let them go back to Chillicothe where they came from.

"You stay here, Steffy," ordered Noel, when they could make neither heads nor tails of what they heard. "I'm goin' back to get Mammy. Wonder what happened to that young un Pappy had posted to warn her?"

"Maybe he's on his way now," said Stephanie.

Noel made his way through the milling crowd toward the gates of the stockade, Stephanie following him.

"Let's ask in the Land Office before you go," Stephanie suggested. "Maybe the surveyor or the deputy'll know for certain what's happened."

In the Land Office they found the surveyor writing in his book as calmly as if nothing had happened. The men standing about the table seemed not to hear the hubbub outside, either. They were buying up Kentucky land. A thousand acres. Two thousand acres. Five hundred acres to a buckskinned settler. Four hundred acres to another. Four thousand acres for a man on the James River. Two thousand acres for a feller in New Jersey.

"Where are the Indians?" asked Noel.

The man from New Jersey turned and eyed him.

"Gone, I hear," he said. "For the moment. You Kentucky buckskins seem to be especially susceptible to the red plague. It ought to make your land cheaper."

Noel's eyes blazed. He set his lips in a thin, tight line while his fingers fidgeted on his rifle. He was burning up inside like a Caroliny tar kiln, and Stephanie half wondered why the smoke didn't come pouring out of him. She caught his sleeve and pulled him to the door.

"Noel," she scolded, "don't be so free and easy with that rifle!"

"Then let that feller stop bein' free and easy with Kentucky," he warned.

Toward the gate they went, Noel smarting under the land buyer's sting. Inside and outside the Land Office were like two different worlds, noticed Stephanie, a make-believe world where a body pretended there was nothing important except grabbing land, a real world on the rim of which six hundred painted red men, spurred on by a handful of British, brandished tomahawks and set fire to new, sweet-smelling cabins, and hauled along a cannon the sight of which scared the liver out of folks. She wondered what a cannon would sound like if the British ever set it off. A thundergust that rocked the hills? The end of the world that Mammy read about in the Book of Revelations?

"Somethin's goin' on here," said Noel, starting toward

the schoolhouse, in front of which a crowd was collecting. "Reckon I'll listen a minute. Might get things straight here."

They edged themselves into the gathering crowd. A man was standing in the doorway, talking. Though his face was the face of a white man, he was rigged out in Indian clothes. He was taller than the men around him, and with his shock of red hair, he put Stephanie in mind of a big bur oak firing up in the fall.

"Who's that?" she whispered.

"Don't know," answered Noel.

"Very well," the man was saying. "The red men have left Kentucky. They're not marching on Harrod's Fort, as I haven't a doubt General Bird intended them to when he landed them on Kentucky soil. They're taking their cannon and leaving this prize in peace, and are heading for the Ohio as fast as they can clear out with their loot and their prisoners. Who's going after them with me?"

Stephanie glanced hurriedly over the crowd. Half a dozen men were volunteering. But many more, looking mighty relieved that the red men had had enough and had gone home, were hemming and hawing, and never raising a hand.

"Right over here," the man was directing the volunteers. "Who else? We need more volunteers than this. Now, if ever, we must strike the enemy, and strike him hard. That's why I've hurried back from the Illinois country to . . ."

"Whew!" whistled Noel softly as he turned wide-open eyes on Stephanie. "Colonel Clark!"

"Are you—sure, Noel?" she whispered, staring at the man.

"Ain't that Colonel Clark?" Noel asked of a buck-skinned man nearby.

"Yep," answered the man. "Looks like he's a-talkin' to the wind, though, for all the volunteers he's a-signin' up."

"Colonel," spoke up a man from the crowd, "I'd like the best in the world to join ye, but this is a job fer Colonel Bowman's milishy. They're paid to do hit. Besides, I got crops a-needin' tendin'. I went hongry last winter, an' I don't aim to again."

Colonel Clark's eyes bored into the man. "There come times when womenfolks can tend corn," he said. "By themselves. And keep the clearings and the cabins. And as for the militia, I'm calling on you to volunteer. It isn't merely a couple of outlying settlements that have been destroyed. It's all Kentucky that's at the mercy of red men."

"You're not talkin' to me, Colonel," spoke up another man. Stephanie recollected she had seen him in the Land Office. Most of the menfolks she had seen in the Land Office were now a part of the curious crowd around the schoolhouse door.

"I got nothin' but land in Kentucky," the man went on. "And when the red men leave for good, the land'll still be here, I reckon. Same goes for the British."

"I ain't even got land," spoke up another. "I come all the way from the Monongahely to buy land and build me a cabin. And what do I find? All the first-rate lands sold to Virginians and bigwigs along the Atlantic seaboard who've never been nigh their claims. Let them that own the land defend it, I say."

It took Colonel Clark a minute to quiet the muttering so that he could be heard.

"If it were only Kentucky land at stake," he said, his dander up, "I wouldn't be asking you to defend it. But the British and the red men want only one thing—to harry the Kentucky settlements till we give up. Make no mistake about it, they'll be back, if we let them come. And if we lose our settlements, we'll lose our liberty, too. If we lose Kentucky, then the British will be at the back door of our nation. And once they wedge the door open, they'll file in. And that will be the end of American freedom. We'll go back then to quitrents and taxation without representation, and all the rest of His Majesty's insults. Don't you see it's more than the red men we fight?" he pleaded with the crowd. "It's the whole system of British tyranny. And no matter how far away from civilization we are out here in the wilderness, we're just as as much a part of a free America as Boston, or New York, or Williamsburg. It's our war as much as it is theirs. War has come to us. We'll have to shoulder our rifles and fight it out."

"All right. I go to fight the Indians and somebody else grabs up the land," objected one listener.

"I came here a-huntin' land, not trouble," muttered another.

"But you found trouble!" snapped Colonel Clark. "When the trouble's over you can go back to hunting land. But while the trouble's on Kentucky soil, you're going to help meet it. Every man of you here, able to carry a rifle."

Without another word, he brushed through the crowd and strode hurriedly in the direction of the Land Office, the curious throng muttering at his back, some of them following at his heels.

From inside the blockhouse Stephanie could hear the colonel's voice snarling like a hornet.

"Close this Land Office! Lock the door!" he snapped at the astonished surveyor.

"Who says to?" the surveyor asked.

"I do!" said Colonel Clark. "And be quick about it!"

The surveyor got to his feet. "But I have no authority to close the Land Office," he said. "And who gives you the authority? Colonel Bowman—he's in command here. He commands the Kentucky County militia."

"And I command Virginia troops," retorted Clark. "And necessity gives me the authority. Put your books away! Lock up!" he commanded the dallying surveyor.

"Post a notice on the door. And you land grabbers, get out of here! No more Kentucky lands will be sold till Kentucky is free. Things have come to a sorry pass," he added, "when men can think of nothing but grabbing up land while life and liberty are snatched from under their very noses!"

Sullenly the land buyers moved out of the blockhouse into the square of the stockade, like dumb critters before a whip.

"If this is the way it's goin' to be," muttered one man, "I mought as well saddle up and ride back to Caroliny."

"Let any man try leaving!" Colonel Clark snapped. "I'm posting sentries on every road out of Harrod's Fort. They have my orders to take the horse and the arms and the powder and lead from any coward who thinks he's running away from Kentucky. This talk of buying up Kentucky land," he spat out disgustedly, "when Kentucky has been stabbed in the back! Kentucky needs every man, every rifle, every keg of powder and every morsel of food as she'll probably never need them again. You're blind that you can't see it. You're blind that you can't see how dark it is all over America!"

His eyes seemed to rest on Stephanie and Noel.

Stephanie nudged Noel. "He's talkin' to us," she whispered.

Noel drew her off to one side and started wrestling with the voice inside him.

"I might join up, Steffy," he said, "only—only—"

"Only Pappy told you to stay home and look after things," she finished for him. "But I can tend the corn as well as you. Colonel Clark said so. Mammy and I'll get along till you come back."

"But Pappy—"

"Don't you recollect what else Pappy told you?" Stephanie interrupted. "He told you no matter what shape that old geezer Frohawk turns up in, you should take care of him."

"What's that got to do with this?" asked Noel.

"This is just Frohawk in another shape," she said, "comin' to claim what he's never sweated for."

Seeing her words made little sense to Noel, Stephanie looked in another direction for arguments.

"Looks like Kentucky's got to do her share before the patriots earn that chance to make their own government," she prodded Noel. "Now's the time you've been waitin' for. You got to use it."

Noel drew her farther from the crowd that they might talk without being overheard. Stephanie could sense the battle going on in him, a hard-fought battle between the forces that bade him stay and keep a promise and the forces that bade him go.

"I—I—" he began.

Stephanie looked at him steadily. "I reckon this is my chance, too, Noel," she said.

After much argument, their plans being made, they set out toward home. Halfway between the Fort and the clearing, they separated, according to plan. Stephanie, on her guard against red men, started hurriedly through the woods toward the Venable clearing. Before the woods closed in about her, however, she turned and looked over her shoulder to see Noel staring after her, as if his mind wasn't yet at the sticking point.

"Skedaddle, Noel," she called, "before Colonel Clark leaves you behind!"

She waited a minute to see him go. Then she herself turned and ran through the woods toward home, realizing for the first time that she was still carrying a kettle filled with sarvice berries.

11. Waiting

THROUGH the woods hurried Stephanie, her eyes searching through the dimness, her ears keen to every snapping twig, every throaty croak of rain crows, every rustle of leaves in the trees, her mind a ferment of explanations to give Bertha about Noel's going away. It was hard to keep her mind on so much at once, and to recollect, to boot, that dark was bound to overtake anybody who loitered overly long in the woods. Already it seemed uncommonly dark, although there must have been two hours of sun in the sky when she and Noel left the Fort.

Oh, but it was scary traipsing by her lonesome through the green gloom of the woods! Along the path she raced, with hair-raising thoughts crowding in on her—thoughts of half-naked, painted red men, egged on by the British, with burning and scalping and stealing in their wild eyes, and paid for their meanness with trinkets and fiery British rum. Thoughts of a loud-mouthed cannon hauled up into a clearing, the look of it terrible as it threatened to belch fire. Thoughts of families, close-knit, being ripped apart, young uns from their mammies, and mammies from pappies. Thoughts of the long road to Detroit. Thoughts of the decrepit and the little whimpering, toddling young uns and the ailing being swiftly clubbed for slowing down the march.

A body could mighty nigh paralyze herself with thinking about red men, Stephanie scolded herself. If she didn't want to go bereft of her senses the way the deputy said some folks did, she had better think about something else—about Colonel Clark burning inside and out like a lightered-knot torch. About Noel. About her Tree of Freedom.

After a while, light began to sift through the woods—grayish, ghostly light with no sun in it. She wasn't far from home now, Stephanie realized, her feet light with relief.

It was with relief, too, that she stopped at the edge

of the clearing and saw the cabin standing as she had left it, and Willie playing on the doorstep with his coon as peaceably as if he had never heard of red men. In the sky dark thunderheads were boiling up, blotting out the sun, and all the leaves on the trees, even on the trembling popple trees, were hanging still as death.

"Mammy!" shouted Willie, spying Stephanie. "Here comes Steffy with the salt!"

"There wasn't any salt, Mammy," Stephanie said, when Bertha met her at the door.

"Well, I reckon you didn't need to lug all them berries home," Bertha told her. "You could have given 'em to somebody that'd 'a' relished 'em. Where's Noel?"

Stephanie wet her lips. She swallowed hard. Why, she scolded herself, hadn't she thought up an answer to that question?

"Willie," she said, "it's goin' to rain, ain't it? You run find Brownie so I can milk her before it storms."

Willie gathered up the coon in his arms and started toward the spring.

"Noel's gone to war, Mammy," said Stephanie, in a low voice.

Bertha stared at her, the tinge of color in her cheeks blanching out. Even her eyes that always looked like velvet looked now as if the pile had been brushed off. She swallowed so hard a body could hear her plainly.

"Gone where?" she asked, her voice a little whisper of hollow sound she made with her lips.

"With Colonel Clark, Mammy," said Stephanie. "To run the Indians and the British back where they came from."

Bertha's hand pressed against the door jamb was drained of color, the knuckles a row of whitened stumps.

"Have red men—"

"They were over on the Lickin' this mornin'," Stephanie told her. "They had a British cannon and every last one of 'em had a rifle the British had put in their hands. And they took Martin's and Ruddell's without ever firin' a shot. That's what we heard at the Fort."

"The folks?" Bertha managed to whisper. "What happened to the folks?"

"The red men are takin' 'em to Detroit," Stephanie told her.

"Lord 'a' mercy!" muttered Bertha, staring at Stephanie. After that, she said not another word.

The sight of her mammy standing in the doorway, pressing her hand against the door jamb as if she needed something steady to hold to, scared Stephanie more than ever the thought of red men had scared her. Bertha looked as if a spell of sickness had been coming over her for a long time, and it had now struck her just when Stephanie was counting on her most. She put Stephanie in mind of a piece of faded white silk. She wouldn't break any place, Stephanie reckoned, when things going on in the wilderness snapped her taut. But all the bright sheen had dulled in her mammy, all the sizing had damped out in the wilderness air. Bertha hadn't looked that way all in a minute, either, Stephanie realized suddenly. It was a wilderness sickness that had been growing on her, like a twisting, winding supplejack getting a stranglehold on a pine tree.

"The Indians have all gone now, Mammy," Stephanie told her, her voice as gentle as if she were quieting a sick young un. "They're scared teetotally to death of Colonel Clark. He's just come back from the Illinois country. Noel and I saw him at the Fort. He's startin' tonight to chase the red men clean out of the country and take their prisoners away from 'em. It was the British that put the red men up to this rascality. They paid 'em to do it. Knives and trinkets and whisky they paid 'em. But Colonel Clark'll make 'em sorry. He needed lots of men to help him, so Noel had to go, too. And while the menfolks are gone, the womenfolks must tend the corn and stave off starvation next winter, Colonel Clark said."

So wrapped up was Stephanie in trying to make her mammy understand, in trying to bring back some color into her face, she didn't notice that Willie hadn't gone for the cow but was hanging around within earshot, lapping up every word she said.

"Are the red men comin' here, Steffy?" he asked fearfully.

"No, Willie, not if Noel can help it."

"Are they, Mammy?" whimpered Willie.

Rob had come to stand beside his mammy in the doorway, his brown eyes burning in his white scared face, while Cassie, clutching her wooden doll in one hand and clinging to Bertha's skirt with the other, puckered up her face.

"Now, listen," Stephanie said to them, her voice loud in her ears, making her feel certain of herself in spite of the fears that gnawed away on the inside of her. "The red men were over on the Lickin' this mornin'. The British got 'em to come. But they've gone now. And Colonel Clark's got up an army to strike out after 'em and give 'em the best whuppin' you ever heard of for their meanness. But what kind of army would it be without Noel? Noel had to go and help, of course."

Cassie smiled up at her, and Willie listened to her as if it was the gospel she was norating. But she couldn't tell off Rob that easily, she realized. She could stand there and norate till the cow came home how not a red straggler was left behind to burn out and scalp and kill cattle and steal horses, and how Colonel Clark and Noel were going to have the Indians and the British whipped in three shakes of a sheep's tail. But Rob was born with horse sense. He eyed her knowingly.

"You'd better go for Brownie, quick, Rob, before the storm breaks," she said, looking at him grimly, as if she dared him to say what was in his mind.

Right away the storm was on them. Forked lightning

danced in the clouds, wind assailed the trees and bent them low, and thundergusts rumbled and bellowed over the clearing and jarred the cabin.

Bertha began herding the young uns inside. This having to do something quickly seemed to put back into her some of the sizing Stephanie's bad news had taken out of her. Not the sheen. Only the sizing.

The rain drove Brownie into the clearing. She bawled at the door of the cabin until Stephanie, during a lull in the downpour, ran out to milk her.

Hurrying into the cabin with her piggin of milk, Stephanie found Bertha trying to cook a bite of supper over the coals in the new fireplace, while rain beat down the chimney and choked the cabin with smoke. Bertha, Stephanie noticed, was trying to make up her mind to broil the last of the turkey meat Noel had brought her.

"Rob can catch some fish tomorrow, Mammy," Stephanie told her, reading her thoughts. "We can live on fish till Noel gets home. Or Pappy'll be here any day now and we'll have fresh meat every meal."

"I could bring in fresh meat if I had a rifle," boasted Rob. "I don't know why Noel had to take his rifle when he went off and left me with all the work to do."

"You couldn't shoot anything with his rifle," Stephanie told him. "You have to be big enough to carry a rifle and aim it before you shoot it."

"I don't know why you think Noel's so all-fired smarter than anybody else!" he shot at her.

Stephanie stared at him through the smoke. She meant to give him a job to do, but changed her mind.

"You come with me, Willie," she said, starting toward the door.

"What to do?" asked Willie.

"Help me bring in all of Pappy's tools," she said.

"What tools?"

"The ax and the adz. And the frow and the grubbin' hoe."

A hoe couldn't be shot like a rifle, she was thinking. But at close range, it could send a man reeling. So could the maul. Better bring inside the cabin and have handy every tool they could find leaning against trees or hooked over the middle log of the west cabin wall.

"Bringin' a hoe in the house is bad luck, Steffy," Rob told her as she made her way through the door, her hands full of rough-handled tools and implements. "You know that."

"It'd be worse luck to leave a hoe out on a night like this," she shot at him. "You fill up every kettle and piggin with water," she ordered. "Have 'em handy in the loft, just in case."

"I don't have to take orders from you," announced Rob.

Now, what in tarnation had got into Rob all of a sudden to fill him so full of sass and make him so bold in the wrong places, Stephanie wondered. Didn't he know how quickly red men could set fire to their cabin, and how water must be handy to douse on the flames? Or didn't he care?

"Go along, Rob," Stephanie heard her mammy saying. "Do as Steffy tells you."

Night brought the wildest storm that Stephanie could ever recollect. The door was bolted with the stout oak bar and double-bolted with a heavy puncheon, and the window was shuttered tight. But through the unchinked cracks in the wall gusts of rain blew and swirled, and rain dripped steadily down the chimney, threatening to blot all life from the red coals Bertha had covered with the ashes. Half a dozen times Stephanie bent over the hearth, anxiously raking through the wet ashes in search of live coals, and recovering them with dry ashes. To let the fire go out now would be a sorry thing, she knew. Not in all of Kentucky County would there be dry kindling enough to start another, she reckoned, after this second epistle of Noah's fresh.

That night the Venable young uns did not climb the ladder to their pallets in the cockloft. Instead, they stretched on a buffalo skin on the floor, facing the door. Bertha lay down with them, on one edge of the skin, with her hand resting on the ax. Stephanie lay on the other edge with her hand on the frow. The hoe, the adz, and the maul she leaned handily against the door jamb.

Until far into the night, the clearing blazed with intermittent light, the rain pounded against the shakes, and the wind whistled and blustered through the trees.

The tall proud crowns of the oak trees bowed down in its wake, and sycamore branches snapped and crackled like whiplashes, and scraped against the cabin roof with sharp rumbling and creaking. It was as if the storm had pre-emption rights to their cabin and their clearing, thought Stephanie, and was trying to drive them out.

As wide awake as a wary barred owl, hooting his eight wild hoots in the rain, Stephanie lay on the pallet listening, sleep as far away as Chiny. At every flash of lightning, she raised on her elbow and peered through the cracks, trying to see what made the noise outside that sounded like somebody running, trying to figure out if the scraping at the chimney was a war-painted body letting himself down into the cabin, or a painter clawing its way into shelter out of the rain.

Beside her Rob and Willie and Cassie slept like three logs, but until the rooster crowed for midnight, she was still straining her ears, still popping up on her elbow every time the lightning, almost played out now, flooded the clearing.

"You better get to sleep, Steffy," Bertha said to her out of the dark.

"I ain't sleepy," Stephanie whispered.

"I reckon the red men ain't no more overly fond of gettin' their feet wet than white folks are," Bertha told her. "Shut your eyes, now."

It was dawn when Stephanie opened her eyes. For a minute she lay awake, feeling logy in every muscle, threatening to doze off again. Then, like a sudden pain, she recollected. She wasn't lying here on a pallet with her hand on a frow for nothing. The rain may have kept red men away in the night, but it wasn't raining now, and this half-light was their favorite time for sneaking in before white folks were astir with all their wits about them.

Quietly she raised on her elbow and gazed through a crack. The wind hadn't died down yet, but nothing that she could see was moving about of its own accord. She turned and looked at Bertha. Her mammy was dozing, her face so pale against the black buffalo pallet it looked like a patch of moonlight on the floor.

Later, as they ate their slim breakfast of eggs, Rob was out of sorts.

"If you ask me," he grumbled, "I'd say we ought to fort."

"Who'd tend the corn, I'd like to know?" Stephanie shot at him. "Varmints?"

When the sun came up over the trees, it seemed to Stephanie the night had gulled them. The rain-drenched clearing gleamed and glistened. Although the corn had been jostled mightily by the wind, nothing else had been changed, nothing disturbed.

Cautiously Stephanie went out into the clearing to milk Brownie, glancing furtively around her with each step. But everything was as it always had been at milking time—Brownie was safely tethered behind the cabin, chewing her cud and switching her tail at flies, the chickens were looking with beady eyes for bugs among the grass, the pigs were loping up from the woods.

Stephanie wondered if what the man they had met on the way to the Fort had said was true—that the red men weren't lurking around in the hills and hollers west of Harrod's Fort. Maybe the runner hadn't come to warn Bertha because he knew she was in no danger. And besides, she figured, a redskin would need a lot of prodding and urging by the British, and promises of many a barrel of rum, to persuade him to put Harrod's Fort between himself and the Ohio River.

"Willie!" she called as she came from milking. "Come here, you and Cassie."

They came running out of the cabin to her.

"Would you two young uns like to be soldiers like Noel, patriot soldiers, and help with the work while he's gone?" she asked.

Willie's eyes shone. He nodded his head. Cassie, watching him, nodded hers, too.

"We have to save this corn patch," she told them, looking down solemnly into their upturned faces. "We've gone without bread a long time now, young uns, but some day this field's goin' to give us bread—roastin' ears, and hoecake, and mush for your milk, and hominy, and corn pone, just like Mammy told you."

Willie squinted at her. He'd been tormented with

hunger so long that the thought of bread set all his senses tingling.

"We'll have bread enough to last all winter," she told them, "if we keep the enemy away from this corn."

"Red men?" whispered Willie, staring at her from frightened eyes.

"Shucks, no!" scoffed Stephanie. "The enemies of the corn don't wear tail feathers and war paint. You know that. The enemies of the corn right now are Brownie and the deer that come snoopin' around every day. Later there'll be crows and squirrels nibblin' and peckin' at the ears. Rob's been keepin' an eye on the enemy, but Rob'll have to help with Noel's work now, and you two'll have to be the soldiers that defend the corn."

She studied their upturned faces.

"Can you?" she asked.

"Sure!" Willie promised her.

"Sure!" echoed Cassie.

"Better stay here close to the cabin door, young uns," she told them. "And if you see a sign of anything movin' in the corn, or in the bushes—anything at all—run call Mammy or me, quick."

She glanced at the Tree of Freedom as she went into the cabin. Looked like before it was big enough to put forth a single blossom it was bearing some of that costly fruit Noel talked about, she said to herself.

Days passed before the Venable young uns could

persuade themselves to talk in their natural voices, or to go about the clearing without shying at every quick sound.

"We could at least go to the Fort and see what's happened," Rob grumbled one day.

"Looks like the red men'd have been here long ago if they'd been comin'," Stephanie assured him. "Anyway, Harrod's Fort's between us and the red men, and recollect how eternal great big it is. You said so, yourself."

"Looks like a body can't waste any more time waitin' for red men," said Bertha. "Not with all we got to do. Rob, you'd better snare me some pigeons this mornin'. Steffy, you hoe the taters and chop out the corn once more. And young uns, look sharp."

There seemed never light enough between sunup and sundown to do all the things that needed doing. The wool had to be carded, and spun on the new wheel Noel had made for Bertha before he went away. All about the clearing a body could hear the song the spinning wheel sang as sometimes Bertha, sometimes Stephanie stood before it, stepping three steps back, and three steps forward, over and over, drawing the roll from the spindle point, then winding the thread on the spindle. It was a little whirring song without a tune, but contented and cheery enough to make Stephanie forget the dark thoughts that bolted through her mind now and then like a pain.

When at last the wool was spun into thick skeins, it had to be dyed. Cautiously through the woods went Stephanie with an unwilling Rob to gather butternut bark for dyeing yellow, and pithy green walnut hulls for dyeing brown, and gray lichens for dyeing a soft rusty shade that put a body in mind of a robin's red breast.

"I don't know why we have to traipse all over creation huntin' dyestuffs," complained Rob, "when Mammy's got no loom to weave cloth on."

"Won't take Pappy and Noel any time to make Mammy a loom, once they get started on it," Stephanie told him.

"How do you know Pappy and Noel are ever comin' back?" asked Rob.

Stephanie didn't answer him for a minute. She thought she heard a queer little tone in his voice—the tone of a young un who wanted mighty bad to see his pappy and who was nursing all kinds of worries in his head and hiding them behind big, sassy talk.

"You can't let yourself think they won't come back, Rob," she said to him gently. "You got to hold on to thinkin' they'll be back as hard as you hold on to a limb when you're skinnin' a cat."

When the dyestuffs were collected and Bertha set her dye pot to boiling, Stephanie rigged out the ash hopper for its winter work, bringing marsh grass and packing it in the bottom of the hopper for a strainer.

"The next time you take ashes out of the fireplace,

Rob," she said, when she finished her work, "you can put them in the hopper. We'll be ready to make hominy as soon as the corn ripens."

Rob, however, didn't answer her. He started down the hill toward the river, plucking a sharp blade of wood grass as he went and blowing a shrill blast on it between his tightly cupped hands. Stephanie looked after him with concern in her face. This blast on a blade of grass had been her answer from him more than once in the last few days, now that they were no longer afraid to breathe because of the red men. For the life of her, she couldn't figure out what ailed Rob. Looked like if it was lonesomeness and worry working at him, he'd take a different turn. Now, if Noel were home, or Jonathan, he wouldn't act so biggety.

Stephanie found her gaze straying often toward the woods through which the trail led to Harrod's Fort. It seemed a queer thing Jonathan wasn't back long ago from Williamsburg, and Noel from the Ohio country. The way Colonel Clark had talked, a body'd think he'd overtake the red men in one night, or two at the utmost, take their prisoners away from them, chase them clean out of Kentucky, and be back at the Fort by suppertime the next day. But Jonathan didn't come, nor Noel.

June faded into July, and the long, sultry days of July crept at a terrapin's pace across the corn patch and the cabin. It was easy enough to fill the tedious hours with work, but it needed noise, thought Stephanie, to drown out the lonesomeness a body felt without Jonathan and Noel, and the anxiety that gnawed at a body when the woods gave never a sign that one or the other of them was on his way home. The deputy said there was a place along the river bottom where a body could holler and raise nine echoes. But this waiting was like calling over and over and over, and raising nary an answer.

Well, Stephanie reckoned, if what they needed was noise, menfolks' noise, there was only one way to get it.

"Rob," she said one morning as he came up from the canebrake carrying two rabbits he had speared with a sharp-pointed stick, "would you help me girdle some trees today?"

"Mammy told Willie and me to catch her some fish for dinner," he said. "Anyway, what you goin' to girdle trees for?"

"Corn and trees can't grow in the same ground," she told him. "And I keep thinkin' how pleased Pappy'll be when he comes home to see the clearin' pushed back into the woods just the same as if he'd been here. It'll look so—so improvement-like."

Rob looked at her, and this time a body could actually see the worry working in his face. He raked his bare toes through the dirt a minute. "Reckon Pappy's ever comin' home, Steffy?" he asked.

For a second her courage failed her—a brief second, until she remembered the Tree of Freedom. "Why, any day now, I look to see Pappy comin' in," she said, "and Noel, too."

"I never saw such a girl for believin' things that ain't there to believe," Rob told her, scornfully. He called Willie, plucked a blade of grass, blew on it, and started toward the river.

Stephanie brought the ax from the cabin, and walked along the edge of the corn patch to the woods on the south side of the clearing. The corn was tall now, so tall that it hid a body standing between the rows. It hid her from the cabin. Maybe she shouldn't venture beyond the corn by her lonesome, even so far as the edge of the woods, she told herself, though never once had they come across a sign of red men. The deputy said whenever red men raided, a few stragglers got separated from the main body and stayed behind to do devilment. But George Rogers Clark had fanned his army out far and wide through the woods like a net, she reckoned, and scooped all the stragglers into it.

She would take the trees as they came, she decided, beginning on an umbrella tree that stood in the corner. Swinging the ax high, she struck the butt first in a downward motion, then upward, cutting through the smooth gray bark into the soft-grained wood. First down, then up, steadily as the harvest fly beating his drum overhead, she swung the ax. But the chips that flew were little chips, not big thick ones such as her pappy or Noel could bite out with the ax. Nor was the noise she made the big, hearty, hefty noise her pappy made girdling trees. Still, it was a noise, and big enough to bring Bertha, holding Cassie by the hand, peering around the edge of the corn.

"Whatever are you doin', Steffy?" Bertha asked.

"I just thought," explained Stephanie, punctuating her words with swings of the ax, "it'd pleasure Pappy to find the land cleared a little farther back."

Girdling trees was slow work, she found. The ax bit easily enough into the soft trunks of the whistlewood trees and the box elders, the bee trees and the Indian bean trees, but the red oaks and the bur oaks, the steel-gray beech trees and the coarse-grained sycamores were tough and stubborn, while from the butt of the hop hornbeam the ax glanced and shivered as if it were trying to bite into iron. It wasn't the girdling that mattered most, however, Stephanie consoled herself when there seemed little to show for her blistered palms and her aching arms. It was noise. And noise aplenty she made.

It wouldn't hurt to have a little noise in the evenings, either, she decided. Not after dark, of course, when a body had to put his whole mind on listening for any sound out of the ordinary. But at sundown, she told herself, it wouldn't hurt to rest from her chopping, and sit on the doorstep, and make a little lively noise.

Going into the cabin, she stood the ax beside the door, climbed the ladder to the loft, and lifted Noel's dulcimer from the peg on which he had hung it.

Willie and Cassie stared at her, wide-eyed, as she sat on the doorstep with the dulcimer across her lap, and cautiously twanged a string.

"Pappy said not to play that dulcimore," Willie told her.

"He didn't tell me not to play it," Stephanie said.

She tried out this string and that one, holding her fingers on the slim neck of the instrument as she had seen Noel hold his. Little by little, awkwardly at first, and so gently it made her think of the wind lolling in the Back Country piny woods, she fashioned a tune.

"Come here, Willie," she called. "You and Cassie."

"What do you want?" asked Willie, as they stood in front of her.

"I'm goin' to learn you and Cassie a ballet," she said. "You sing with me now.

> "All in a misty mornin',
> Cloudy was the weather,
> I meetin' with an old man
> Clothed all in leather."

She sang softly as she plucked the strings. The sound her voice made and the sound the strings made weren't always the same sound, but it was a good sound, she decided. Willie and Cassie, with eyes fastened on her, and with smiles of pleasure spreading over their faces, mumbled the words uncertainly after her.

"Mammy!" called Steffy as Bertha came up from the

spring house with a piggin of milk. "Listen to this. Sing, now, young uns."

Boldly she plucked the strings this time, and the three of them raised their voices.

> "All in a misty mornin',
> Cloudy was the weather,
> I meetin' with an old man
> Clothed all in leather.
> With ne'er a shirt upon his back,
> But wool unto his skin,
> With how d'ye do,
> And how d'ye do,
> And how d'ye do again."

Now and then Stephanie glanced at her mammy's face. Maybe the sound of singing would make the tautness in her mammy give a little, she hoped, would untie some of the knots inside her worried mind. But she wasn't prepared for the thing Bertha did at that moment.

Bertha set the piggin on the hominy block as if she aimed to rest herself while she listened. First, she smiled. When the young uns reached the chorus and began to curtsey stiffly to each other as Stephanie had taught them, she laughed aloud. That was just like a miracle in the old Huguenot Bible, thought Stephanie. But when they started on the second verse, Bertha pitched in and sang it with them, keeping time with her foot like a fiddler at a shindig.

"I went a little further
And there I met a maid,
Was goin' then a-milkin',
A-milkin', sir, she said.
Then I began to compliment,
And she began to sing,
With how d'ye do,
And how d'ye do,
And how d'ye do again."

"Tomorrow, young uns," Stephanie said to Willie and Cassie, as they finished the song, "I'll learn you a ballet called 'Here Come Three Dukes a-Ridin'.' "

The next day, decided Bertha, the beans were ripe for picking. Not a great many of them, of course, but enough for a mess for dinner. All morning long she boiled them over a fire in the fireplace, seasoning them with pigeon meat.

"I reckon they won't hardly taste like beans," Bertha complained, "without salt meat for seasonin'. And no salt either. Bear's meat would do if we had it."

A sudden worry lodged in Stephanie's mind. It had been almost a month since Noel had gone away. Supposing they had no rifle to kill deer and bears for the winter's meat, and no one to shoot it.

Oh, well! They'd find some way. Jason Pigot had a rifle. Rob could go across the river to Jason's cabin, and ask him to bring the Venables a bear when he went hunting. Looked like the Pigots would come over some time, she thought to herself.

Despite the bland seasoning and the lack of salt, the beans were enough to put new life into a body. A dozen times while they were boiling, the young uns lifted the kettle lid to sniff. But when, finally, Bertha dished them out and the young uns stood ready for them around the table, Stephanie laid her sassafras fork back on her wooden plate, the beans untouched.

"What's the matter, Steffy?" asked Bertha. "Don't they taste good?"

"I was just thinkin', Mammy," explained Stephanie. "Looks like the first beans'd be a fittin' present to take to Lonesome Tilly. I could take him part of mine," she added. "I don't want nearly so many."

"You can take some of mine, too," said Bertha.

Stephanie glanced at Bertha's plate. Only a little portion of broken beans lay on it. The rest she had given to the young uns.

"Mine'll be enough without yours," Stephanie told her.

But Bertha had her way. "Looks like I've done without beans so long, I've lost my taste for 'em. Hurry up, young uns. As soon as you finish, we'll all go to see Lonesome Tilly."

They set out through the woods, Stephanie leading the way, carrying the ax on her shoulder. Rob carried the frow. Bertha carried the grubbing hoe in one hand and the plate of beans in the other, while Cassie and Willie filled up the gaps in the line.

Their feet on the springy ground were as noiseless as the padded feet of varmints. Down through the May apple bed they went, pulling the mawkish apples that were ripening now, and eating them as they walked; through undergrowth; through lacy ferns that brushed softly against their ankles and tickled their bare legs.

After half an hour Stephanie stopped and peered through the underbrush at the grassy knoll held in the elbow of the stream, but nowhere was the strange old man to be seen. Only one thing could they see moving about the knoll, a lone bee that lit on a cardinal flower rearing its long stalk beside the stream, and set its scattered velvety blossoms to trembling like little fires glowing in the green shade.

"We'll cross over and sit down and wait," said Bertha.

They had not sat long on the knoll facing the tiny cabin when the bushes beside it parted, and Lonesome Tilly peered through at them, raking them with surprised, questioning eyes.

Cassie clutched Bertha's skirt and Willie moved closer to her.

Bertha held out the plate of beans.

"We brought you somethin', Tilly," she said. "It's our first beans. We wanted you to have some."

He hesitated a minute. Slowly the dark trouble in his

heifer-like eyes turned first to trust, then, as they came finally to rest on Willie, to pleasure. He shuffled forward, took the plate from Bertha's hand, made the hint of a bow with his shaggy head, then disappeared inside his cabin.

"Wonder what he's aimin' to do?" whispered Rob, staring after the old man.

"Let's go, Mammy!" begged Willie. "Let's go before he comes back."

"Can't he say one little bitty word?" whispered Cassie. "Nary one?"

At that moment Lonesome Tilly came out of the cabin, carrying the plate of beans in one hand, and in the other a popple leaf basket filled with big frosty-blue huckleberries.

He handed the basket to Bertha, then sat down on the grass a little distance from her. He picked up a fork full of the beans, but before putting them in his mouth, he motioned Bertha to taste the huckleberries and to pass them to the young uns.

It was a queer feast they ate there on the knoll, with no one talking but Bertha. First, she said to Lonesome Tilly she had never tasted such sweet huckleberries, and if she only had some pig's lard flavored with laurel leaves and some wheat flour and some maple sugar, she would make him a huckleberry pie. When Tilly made no answer to that, she told him she noticed his corn growing in a patch back of his cabin was higher than the Venables' corn, and it looked as if he might be having roasting ears soon. When Tilly still made no answer, Bertha said to Cassie the huckleberries were a match for her eyes, and to Willie that they would have to look for huckleberries on the way home.

The Venable young uns, however, had no more than Lonesome Tilly to say to Bertha. In awe of the silent old man, they ate their berries in silence, too, while their sheepish eyes studied the knoll and the cabin, and the corn patch beyond.

When Lonesome Tilly had finished the beans, he stood up and handed the plate to Bertha, and the Venables, having finished the huckleberries, rose to go.

"Come over soon," Bertha said to Lonesome Tilly.

He did not move, but stood watching them as they crossed the little run that separated the knoll from the woods.

Willie kept looking back as long as he could get a glimpse of Lonesome Tilly.

"I wish he'd talk," he said.

"He ha'nts me," declared Rob.

"Reckon we'll ever know why he won't talk, Mammy?" asked Willie.

"Chances are, we won't," Bertha told him. "Apt as not, we'll never know much of anything about him—where he came from, or why he wanted to live out here with varmints and red men 'stid of with his kinfolks, or what ails him that he can't talk. You'll just have to take Lonesome Tilly the way you find him, young uns, and ask no questions."

They trudged on a distance in silence.

"You'll meet up with lots of queer folks in your lifetime, young uns," Bertha said to them. "And not all of 'em that talk say words to match what they're thinkin'. But you'll grow wise as you grow old, and then you'll learn that what folks are is in their faces. Take Lonesome Tilly's face, now. Main thing I see in it is hurt, and starvation—starvation a lot deeper than a body's hunger for the first beans."

They stopped to watch a squirrel building a nest in the crotch of an oak tree.

"You don't know it now, young uns," said Bertha, "but that sort of starvation can seal a body up airtight, and a poor soul can never find his way out 'cept through folks' human kindness."

It was sundown when they reached their clearing, for they had rambled through the woods looking for huckleberries. When they finished their chores, Stephanie, with her mind on Lonesome Tilly, took down Noel's dulcimer, sat on the doorstep, and sang lonesome words to fit a sad, lonesome tune she twanged on the strings.

> "The poor soul sat sighing by a sycamore tree;
>
> Sing willow, willow, willow!

With his hand in his bosom, and his head upon his knee;
Oh! Willow, willow, willow, willow,
Oh! Willow, willow, willow, willow,
Shall my garland be!
Sing all a green willow, willow, willow, willow,
Ah, me! The green willow must my garland be!"

12. "Indians!"

AS SOON as the light faded that night, Bertha bolted the door and the Venables lay down on the buffalo skin as they had every night since Noel went away, Bertha on one edge with her hand on the ax, Stephanie on the other edge with her hand on the frow. But Rob had no sooner lain down than he got up again.

"I'm might' nigh smothered to death," he complained, "sleepin' between so many womenfolks."

Stephanie could hear him stumbling around over the puncheon floor, feeling his way in the dark.

"Where do you aim to sleep, then?" she asked.

"In the loft," he said. "On my own pallet. Where I can have a little elbow room."

Suppose red men came, thought Stephanie. It would take time, precious time they could ill spare, to go up the ladder and wake Rob.

"Why don't you fix a pallet down here, Rob?" she asked. "You can sleep on it by yourself."

"Why can't I sleep in the loft, I'd like to know?" he grumbled.

"Rob, bring your pallet down here," Bertha told him quietly.

Rob stumbled up the ladder. Though Stephanie could not see him, she knew his face was sulky, his arms were dangling out of his coarse linsey shirtsleeves, and his short breeches were well above the knees of his lanky legs. Why, Rob wasn't a little shaver any more, Stephanie realized. He was growing as lank as bracken in a thicket. Apt as not, he was growing the same way on the inside, too, growing bigger than the notions and the ways he had when he was a young un, pushing out at everything, trying to make room for himself, and getting mad as a hornet at anybody who tried to keep him cooped up where he'd been all his life.

"Rob," she said, when he backed down the ladder with an old blanket, "why don't you lay your pallet over there by the chimney? That's a place somebody ought to be handy to, don't you s'pose? You can sleep with the maul."

After a while the cabin grew quiet. Cassie and Willie fell asleep almost before they could nestle their bodies down into the rough places in the floor, and Bertha and Rob were asleep soon afterwards. Sleep did not come so easily to Stephanie, however. It was crowded to one side by uneasy wonderings—what had happened to her pappy, why didn't Noel come back, what was a body to do with Rob who was plainly getting too big for his breeches, what stark, fearful thing had fashioned the strange face and the stranger ways of Lonesome Tilly, what had become of Frohawk?

She yawned, and dozed, waked up, listened, yawned, and dozed, and waked up. She wondered what time it was. It might be midnight, but she hadn't heard the rooster crow.

Something in the clearing moved.

Stephanie lay as still as a shadow, listening. Something, somebody had bumped into the hominy sweep, she knew.

Wide awake, her eyes stared into the darkness. Her heart pounded like the pestle in the hominy block as she got to her feet.

Gripping the frow, she laid her ear against a crack between the logs. After a minute she heard the sound again. Somebody, a whole passel of folks, it sounded like, were fumbling their way under and around the sweep.

Stephanie never knew how she got to her mammy's

side. She remembered only that she mustn't wake Willie and Cassie. Young uns might fret and whimper and be a hindrance.

"Mammy!" she whispered, close to Bertha's ear. "Wake up!"

She tiptoed across the floor in the direction of Rob's pallet. Her hands, cold with fright, felt for his shoulder. She shook him like a dog shaking a cat.

"Wake up, Rob! Get up! Quick! Get the maul!"

She didn't know her own voice, it sounded so almighty skittish.

The three of them tiptoed to the door. Close together they huddled, waiting, the ax, the frow, and the maul ready.

They could hear footsteps now, hurrying footsteps, fumbling in the dark, making straight for the cabin door.

"Don't move, young uns," whispered Bertha. "They'll try to prize the door down. When one of 'em gets his head in, stand back and hack hard."

It warmed some of the fright out of Stephanie to hear her mammy taking command like a general. Rob brushed against her, feeling out the rough handle of the maul with his fingers. He put his fingers to his mouth and wet them with spit, like a man.

A hand fumbled at the door.

Stephanie gripped the frow handle, raised the frow to strike.

"Jonathan!" a deep voice whispered loudly outside the door.

The three waited.

"Jonathan Venable!" the whisper came again, hoarse and rasping for breath.

Finally Bertha spoke.

"Who's a-callin' Jonathan?" she asked.

"Me," the voice answered. "Jason Pigot. An' Prissie an' the young uns. Let us in, quick, Berthy!"

Stephanie moved to unbolt the door, but Bertha touched her arm. Still they waited.

"Prissie," said Bertha, talking low in her throat, "say somethin' in your own voice."

"Lord 'a' mercy, let us in quick, Berthy!" whimpered Prissie.

Her voice froze Stephanie. It held all the terror of the wilderness corked up and ready to spout over.

As quickly as they could, Stephanie and Rob unbolted the door. Jason and Prissie pushed the Pigot young uns inside and crowded in after them, stumbling over one another in their hurry.

"Lordy, Berthy, the red men are on a rampage!" Jason jerked out in a tight voice. He fumbled for the puncheon with which the door had been double-bolted and shoved it hard against the door. "Didn't you see the fire?"

"What fire?" asked Bertha.

"The whole sky's lit up, like Jedgment Day!" said Jason. "Whar's Jonathan? Ain't he here?"

"He's been gone more'n a month," Bertha told him.

"Jonathan has?" Jason's voice was full of concern. "Whar'd he go to?"

"To Williamsburg. Expressin' for Colonel Bowman," Bertha said.

"Then why didn't you let a body know?" Jason scolded. "Who is here?"

"Rob and Steffy," Bertha said. "And the little young uns. They're asleep here on the floor. Mind you don't trample 'em."

"Noel?" asked Jason. "Whar's Noel? Ain't he here?"

"He's with Colonel Clark," Bertha told him.

"Consarn!" Jason muttered between his teeth. "Of all the nights on earth for menfolks to be away from home!"

Prissie began to cry, smothering little whimpering noises in her throat. A body could tell the tears were rolling down her cheeks like a salty fresh.

"Hit's north of us a little—little ways," she sobbed. "The claim next to ourn. Some new folks cleared there a month ago. Hit—hit's their place a-burnin' up. Us Pigots—Pigots are next."

Prissie was shaking like the queer popple trees that shake all the time—the popple trees that Bertha said Jesus's cross was made of.

"Looky!" said Jason. "You can see the fire from here. Look through the cracks by the chimney."

They huddled together in the west end of the cabin, in the chimney corner, and peered through the cracks. The sky over the place where the Pigots allowed the new settlers had raised their cabin looked like a great wide meadow full of blazing bee balm. It didn't look like fire, said Rob. It looked like blood.

"We'd better get to the Fort, Berthy. Quick," said Jason.

"I'll wake up Cassie and Willie," offered Rob.

Bertha made no move to get ready.

"Prissie," she asked, "can you make it to the Fort?"

"Looks like—I can't go one—one step further, Berthy," she sobbed, trying not to make a noise. "Not even—not even if a tomahawk was—was hangin' over my head."

"Then we won't go," said Bertha. "I reckon we're a sight safer takin' our chances here than traipsin' four miles through the woods in the pitch dark with all these young uns."

She felt for Prissie's hand.

"Here, Prissie," she said. "Sit down on my bed. Jason, you've got a rifle. You and Steffy can guard the door. Rob, you stay by the chimney. Where're the young uns?"

One by one Bertha found the three Pigot young uns and set them on the bed beside Prissie. She picked up

Willie and Cassie from the floor and laid them on the bed beside the Pigots. Then she took up the buffalo skin.

Stephanie could hear her moving about the cabin.

"What're you doin', Mammy?" she asked.

"I aim to put all five young uns in the tater hole. On the buffalo skin," said Bertha. "If the red men come, we'll hide the young uns with the puncheons, and fight it out."

Jason put in to arguing all over again that they should go to the Fort while there was time. It was as big a piece of foolishness as a body had ever dreamed of to be so stubborn about forting.

"If you go fortin', you go without Prissie," Bertha told him sharply. "Anyhow," she added, "mightn't be red men at all. It might be a cabin a-burnin' up from folks' own carelessness. Carelessness has lit as many fires in the wilderness, I reckon, as red men ever did."

When Bertha got the five young uns settled on the buffalo skin in the potato hole, she felt her way to the fireboard and took from it the hickory knitting needles Noel had whittled for her, and a skein of thread dyed brown with walnut hulls.

"Here," she said, laying them in Prissie's hands. "There's nothin' like doin' somethin' with your hands to work the worry out of a body. You knit, Prissie, and the rest of us'll watch. Start knittin' a pair of man-sized socks. I have a mind to give 'em to Lonesome Tilly."

13. Chinking Talk

UNTIL the sun began to edge its way over the clearing, the watchers stood at their posts, every now and then gazing anxiously through the cracks at the western sky from which the red glow slowly faded. Daylight found Prissie still at her knitting. All night long her needles had clicked in the dark like a ticking beetle.

"I'm a-thinkin' I'd better go into the Fort," announced Jason, "soon's I eat a bite, an' see what I can learn. Hit mought 'a' been carelessness that set the cabin afire, 'stid of the red men, like you said, Berthy."

"But it mought 'a' been red men," Prissie told him. "You won't—stay till after dark?" she begged, having no more shame than a young un about parading her fears.

It was good to hear voices again, speaking out loud, even though they were taut and sharp at the edges, and bore signs of the sleepless, anxious night.

"Naw," promised Jason. "I'll be right back, Prissie, soon as I hear somethin'."

Jason cut out through the woods in the direction of the Fort as soon as he had eaten his breakfast, but a body could see he took no relish in traipsing off by his lonesome. Instead of carrying his rifle in the hollow of his shoulder, he carried it in both hands as he walked warily along. He didn't aim to be taken unawares, he said.

It was almost dark when he came hurrying out of the woods.

"Closer to home I got," he explained, "the more hit seemed like somethin' or other was a-crowdin' me in the bushes."

Prissie stared at him helplessly, afraid to ask what he knew, afraid not to ask.

"Looks like—like you didn't get back as soon as you thought for," she said to him, weakly.

"I was waitin' for the searchin' party to get back," explained Jason. "They'd set out before I got there."

The Venables and the Pigots crowded together in the cabin, the door bolted securely. Some of them sat on Bertha's bed, some on the three-legged stools, while the little boys squatted on their haunches, waiting for Jason to go ahead and tell all he knew.

"Family by the name of Isom had moved out there a month ago, they said. Man an' his wife, an' two brothers of his'n. Striplin's, folks said. Had a cabin built an' trees girdled, goin' to do some late fall plantin'. Well, looks like they didn't get much for their pains. Searchin' party couldn't find hair nor hide of 'em."

"What did they find, Jason?" asked Bertha.

"Nothin'," he said. "Not a solitary thing to lead a body to 'em, if they're still alive. Jist a heap of red hot coals of fire whar the cabin used to stand."

"Maybe their cabin caught fire from the chimney," Stephanie suggested. "Maybe they're just campin' out till they can raise a new cabin."

Jason sat silent a minute.

"That ain't exactly what I make of a searchin' party not bein' able to find hair nor hide of 'em," he said at last. "Looks like hit's a tale with a sorrier endin'. The searchin' party did stumble on one clue at the edge of the clearin'," he added. "But hit was a slim un. I traded some powder for hit."

He took from his shirt bosom a little bitty Bird Head pistol no longer than the span of his hand and held it up in the dim light for them to see. Rob bent close to study it.

"Hit's exactly the same notion as a flint lock rifle," Jason said, " 'ceptin' hit's pint size. An' this here silver plate on the handle," he said, pointing to the spot of metal on which the dim light fell, "has got some feller's initials on hit. 'M. R. B.' some feller at the Fort with book learnin' told me. But I reckon M. R. B. has rammed home his last charge of powder through this little trick of a barrel. Here, Rob," he said, handing the pistol to him, "looks like you've took a shine to this purty. You mought as well have hit for keeps. 'Twon't do me no good. Don't reckon a man could shoot much with hit 'cept his own hand, mebbe, when hit backfires."

Rob's joy in his possession was smothered quickly, however.

"You put that pistol up on the fireboard, Rob," Bertha ordered, "and leave it there." Sensing his disappointment, she added, "Till I say you can shoot it. With two of our menfolks gone, I reckon I don't care to have the last un tearin' his hand to smithereens with a thing like that. Did you—you didn't hear any word of Jonathan, Jason?"

"Nary a word, Berthy. I shore didn't."

"Did you hear any word of Colonel Clark? And Noel?" asked Stephanie.

Jason drew a deep breath.

"Colonel Clark didn't find hit so all-fired easy to get recruits for his campaign against the red men an' the British," he said. "Know whar he's been right up until lately? An' Noel with him? Jist a-layin' around in the Fort at the Falls on Corn Island tryin' to get folks to join up. Oh, Noel, they say he was busy enough, all right," Jason hurried to add when silence hard as stone greeted his news. "Folks say Colonel Clark took a mighty shine to him. Had him out a-helpin' to recruit."

"Where are they now?" asked Stephanie.

"They never left the mouth of the Lickin' till the first day of August, folks said," Jason told her. "Then when they got across the Ohio, Clark stopped long enough to build a blockhouse there. Now they say he's finally got around to chasin' the Indians after givin' the rascals plenty of time to get clean away."

Stephanie got up from the stool where she was sitting and began raking ashes over the coals of fire left from cooking supper. She didn't like Jason's talk of Noel and Colonel Clark. She didn't like the ugly tone in his voice, either. Apt as not, Jason wasn't telling all he knew. At least, he wasn't telling all he thought.

" 'Pon my word, Steffy!" said Jason suddenly. "I plumb forgot I had a present for you."

He reached inside his shirt bosom and took out a small object and handed it to her. "The surveyor, he said some preacher feller brung this book to Noel,"

Jason explained. "An' when I told him Noel was traipsin' around the Ohio country, he 'lowed he'd send hit to you. Said you'd know what to do with hit."

Stephanie almost snatched the book from him in her haste to see it. She scanned longingly the words printed on the back of it, then uncovered the coals and laid a dry chip on them, and opened the book in front of the blaze. But the words were meaningless to her. Only the book itself had meaning. It was a thing that would light a thousand candles in Noel's eyes when he came home.

No sooner had Jason finished his tale than Bertha began putting Prissie to bed, and giving her a noggin of stout hot tea brewed of white slippery elm bark. Prissie sat on the edge of the bed sipping the tea and, in the flickering light cast by the chip Stephanie had laid on the fire, looking clean out of her head with terror of the dark night. It was just such unbridled fear as that, Stephanie thought, that might have turned Lonesome Tilly into a queer woodsy critter. Supposing, she said to herself, Prissie Pigot lost her reason in the night? But that, she scolded herself, was no proper thought to take along with a body into a dark night.

Bertha began settling the young uns on the pallet beside the potato hole.

"Steffy, I reckon you and Rob can watch till the rooster crows for midnight," she said. "Jason and I'll get up then and watch till daylight."

"I can watch, too," pleaded Prissie, afraid to go to sleep.

"You leave the listenin' to the rest of us tonight, Prissie," Bertha soothed her. "You curl up there on the bed now and go to sleep. You need to get your strength back for what's a-comin'."

Drawing the stools up near the door, Stephanie and Rob sat down on them and began their watch, whispering to each other now and then to keep themselves awake, peering often through the cracks into the dark clearing.

Prissie Pigot jerked so hard in her sleep she shook the bed, and every little while she cried out like a young un that's been whipped.

"We've got a job tomorrow, Rob," Stephanie whispered.

"What?" he asked.

"Chinkin'. We got to chink this whole cabin, you and me," she told him.

"You and me!" snorted Rob. "Why, Steffy, that'd take us a month. Two months. It'd take us a whole month of Sundays."

"We'll begin, anyway. Tomorrow," she told him.

"Why don't we wait till Pappy comes home?" asked Rob.

"Pappy might—get home awful late," she explained. "It'll be a whole sight safer when the holes are all chinked up, and, besides, the night air's bad for a body. Even if it takes us a month of Christmases," she added, when Rob grunted to show what he thought of her notions, "we'll begin."

"What'll we chink with, I'd like to know?" he asked. "You're not a-sendin' me after marsh grass."

"There's plenty of chinkin' right here in the clearin', I reckon," she told him. "Chips and such."

"Even the clearin' ain't safe, Steffy," he complained. "If the red men got as close as Isom's cabin, they're just too close to the Venable clearin' to be lettin' on like there's no danger."

"You don't know it was Indians at Isoms'," she said.

"You don't know it wasn't," he sassed back at her.

When the morning chores were finished, Stephanie took a look at the cabin walls, and stifled a sigh. The cabin had never seemed so eternal great big, the cracks between the logs so like a wide yawn when a body is sleepy. They'd begin at the bottom crack, she announced.

"Let Willie and Cassie and the Pigot young uns gather chips," Rob told her. "Somebody's got to watch for red men. I'll do the watchin'. We'll die of old age before we get this done," he added.

"You may," Stephanie told him tartly. "I don't aim to."

She turned from studying the cracks and looked at Rob.

"When we get the chinkin' done, Rob, I'll help you

catch some butterflies and mount 'em," she promised.

"Willie can catch the butterflies from now on, I reckon," said Rob.

Stephanie felt crushed, like an apple somebody has stepped on with a heavy foot.

"Oh, come on, Rob," she begged. "It won't always be this hard. You got to look ahead a little."

"You sound just like Noel," Rob told her. "You're gettin' to be as bad at drummin' up big notions as he ever was."

"You shut up about Noel," she ordered. "Else I'll duck you in daubin'."

When Jason heard what they planned to do, he told Prissie the Pigots might as well stay a day or two longer, and he'd help with the chinking. By that time, if the red men hadn't showed up, chances were they'd gone back across the Ohio where they belonged.

With Rob and Stephanie, he went to the river for clay, the three of them lugging kettles full of the heavy daubing up the hill. Then he cut down saplings to lodge in the cracks while the young uns gathered chips to mix with the clay. All morning Jason and Stephanie worked, filling the cracks, making the cabin warm against winter. And dark. It was a sight how dark the cabin was getting to be, now that the cracks were being filled with daubing.

"Too bad Noel couldn't 'a' been here doin' somethin' useful like this all the time he was tryin' to drum up an army for Colonel Clark," Jason told Stephanie, as he smoothed the daubing into a crack with a paddle he had whittled out of a piece of ash.

Stephanie had nothing to say to that. She thought a-plenty. A body could read what she was thinking by the straight line of her lips, by the clouding of her blue eyes, by the way she worked like ten beavers.

"Tell you one thing, Steffy," Jason went on, glad of a chance to clear his chest of a matter or two. "Men think twice afore they pitch in an' fight these days. Here we been a-fightin' the British five years—five long, endurin' years, an' ever' day we retreat jist a little bit farther from victory. Way the fightin's goin' now, some army's goin' to draw up in a straight line one of these days, an' pass over their guns. An' from the looks of things, hit ain't a-goin' to be the British."

Still Stephanie didn't answer.

Jason daubed a while longer, then let into whistling.

"Hit's too bad Noel ever tuck up with Clark," he said, at the end of a tune. "Clark's all right. But he ain't on the winnin' side. An' lots of folks, Steffy, who ain't on the winnin' side, apt as not, 'll end up in jail somewhars for their pains."

Still no rise out of Stephanie. Jason took a kettle and went to the river bank for more clay.

"If you know what I mean, Steffy," he said, when he set to work again, "Noel'd 'a' done a sight better if he'd stayed home an' minded his business."

Stephanie looked at him, her chicory blue eyes crackling with anger. "Noel was mindin' his business, Jason Pigot!" she snapped.

Stephanie was glad when, the next morning, the Pigots left. Oh, she knew she was beholden to Jason Pigot. He and his rifle had stood between the Venables and the red men. And for all her big notions, Jason had done most of the chinking.

But to have to listen to him claiming scurrilous things about Noel was worse than eating puckery persimmons.

14. Frohawk Again

AS SOON as the Pigots had gone, Stephanie took the ax and went cautiously to girdle trees, but her eyes kept straying in the direction of Harrod's Fort. The woods to the east were enough to drive a body out of her wits, she thought, hiding as they did behind their dark, green curtain the fate that had overtaken her pappy and Noel. More than two months ago the woods had swallowed up Jonathan. Surely, if ever he was coming home from Williamsburg, he ought to be home now. It looked like one of these days a body would have to quit pretending, and say to herself he would never come back again. Something was keeping him forever.

She let the ax head rest on the ground, and leaned her weight on the handle. A hot August wind was fanning the dark green leaves, a mocking wind that plagued her with the things it hinted but kept secret from her.

Lifting the hem of her skirt, Stephanie buried her face in it, and cried and cried.

After a long time, she stopped her sobbing, and wiped her red, swollen eyes on her skirt. It was no use to watch for her pappy any longer, she told herself, turning to the east woods once more as if to say to the mocking wind that she understood.

Her eyes didn't see the woods, however. They fell instead on the Tree of Freedom that grew between the woods and the tasseling corn. It was no longer a gray-green sprig, but a sturdy whip of a sapling beginning to branch, its dark green glossy leaves shining in the sun. It seemed to mock her, too, but not as the woods and the wind in the tree crowns mocked her. It shamed her that she stood there crying into her skirt. Hadn't she made a promise to Noel that she would take his place about the clearing, that on the day he came home he would find things done in their season, it seemed to say to her.

Noel would be mighty ashamed of her if he could see

her now, she told herself. So would Jonathan. And what would Grandmammy Linney think if she could peep through the corn and catch her standing there with tears running down her face like a fresh? And Bertha, she reckoned, would feel plumb deserted at such a sorry sight.

Setting her mouth grimly, she lifted the ax and whacked at a tree with all her might.

The crying made her feel better. The ax, she realized, felt lighter as she made up her mind to watch the woods a while longer for her pappy, and to keep her promise to Noel no matter what dark shadow fell across the clearing.

She tried to imagine the look in Noel's face when he saw the book Jason had brought from the preacher feller. It must be *Pilgrim's Progress,* she decided. Noel had told her the story as Uncle Lucien had told it to him, and the picture in the front of the book of a man trudging along toward the sun, with a book in one hand from which he read and a staff in the other with which he walked, and with three birds flying along overhead to keep him company, seemed to fit the story.

In the evenings Willie and Cassie stood around the doorstep begging Stephanie to play the dulcimer, but she spent part of the time poring over the pages of the book. Noel would read it to her when he came home, she told herself. But what if Noel didn't come for a long, long time?

Her helplessness pricked her like a thorn. If Noel didn't come soon to read the book to her, she'd learn to read it herself, she decided.

"Mammy," she begged, holding the book open before Bertha, "can't you help me read this?"

"I wish I could, honey," Bertha said gently, understanding the hunger in the blue eyes. "I could, I reckon, if it was French. But English words I never learned."

"Nary a one?"

"Nary a one," said Bertha.

She went into the cabin to light the fire for cooking supper, but when she got it burning, she came out again.

"I reckon I could teach you your ABC's, Steffy," she said. "They're the same, whether you're readin' in French or in English. Knowin' your ABC's won't tell you exactly what the words are, but it'll help. And maybe you can ferret out the words yourself, once you know how to spell 'em."

Willie and Cassie crowded around, peering over the edges of the book, as Bertha pointed out the letters, beginning with A.

"Reckon a body has to write 'em, actually to learn 'em," she said. "And maybe together we can make out some of the words."

"I wish I had a page of paper out of the surveyor's book," sighed Stephanie, "and his goose quill pen and some of his pokeberry ink."

But a page of paper, she decided, was a flimsy excuse

to stand between her and her knowledge of the ABC's. Finding a big chip in the clearing, she whittled it smooth with Rob's knife, then found a charred piece of wood, and began copying the letters. As long as she could see, she sat on the doorstep making rings and curlycues, and little bitty pothooks and ash hoppers, whittling them off, and making them again. Cassie and Willie bent over her, watching her progress, as pleased as if she were playing the dulcimer.

Stephanie reckoned she knew how a seed felt now, its dry, hard skin bursting with the stirring of a pale green shoot feeling its way outward and upward through the dark earth to the sunshine. She felt the same way. A tender green shoot of knowing how to read was breaking right through the dark brown dullness that was her mind, and making its way to the light. Some day she could read anything she could lay hands on—books, kings' grants of land, tax laws, land laws, anything a body held out to her, she would step right up and read it off. Why, when Noel came home, she reckoned she'd read *Pilgrim's Progress* to him, instead of listening to him read it to her.

A week later Jason Pigot came tearing up the hill from the river, bareheaded and barefooted, his eyes like the eyes of somebody who has met a ha'nt in the woods. Stephanie, milking the cow in a corner of the clearing, stared after him.

"What's the matter, Jason?" she called.

Jason, however, did not hear her.

Setting down her piggin, Stephanie hurried toward the cabin.

"Berthy," she heard Jason panting at the door. "Prissie says—can you come—right away quick?"

Bertha was spinning, the big wheel whirring hard against the nippy autumn days that would be on them before long now. She stopped her pacing back and forth, and put her hand on the wheel to slow it.

"I was thinkin' it was time you came," she said.

Deftly she rolled her thread up and laid it on the standard, then reached for her bonnet that hung on a peg on the wall.

"How's Prissie doin'?" she asked.

"She's mighty bad off, Berthy," Jason answered, begging her with his panicky voice to be quick.

"You don't s'pose . . ."

Bertha hesitated a minute in the doorway, trying to settle some matter in her mind.

"Is it safe, Jason, do you reckon, to leave the young uns here?" she asked. "Or had I better take 'em all along?"

"There ain't no signs of red men about, Berthy, if that's what you mean," he said. "Not since the Isoms got scalped."

"Run hunt Cassie," Bertha said to Steffy. "I'll take

her with me, I reckon. Tell Rob to help you around the clearin' while I'm gone, and tell Willie to pick me up some shelly bark. I'll try to get back before dark."

Stephanie stared at her mammy, trying to figure out the reason for her great haste.

"Prissie Pigot's birthin' a baby, Steffy," Bertha said.

When they had gone, Stephanie took her grubbing hoe and went into the corn. The corn itself needed no more hoeing. She and Rob had laid it by and had left it to ripen in its own good time. But the tree sprouts were like ghosts that couldn't be laid. No sooner was one grubbed out than another shot up.

Soon Willie and Rob came up the hill from the river with three big-mouthed catfish strung on a twig.

"What did Jason want?" asked Rob.

"Mammy," said Stephanie. "Prissie's mighty poorly. Mammy said for you to help me in the corn, Rob, and for you to scout around and find her some shelly bark, Willie."

"I got to clean these fish," announced Rob.

"Just lay 'em in the river," Stephanie told him. "Lay a big rock on the end of the twig to weight it down. Then we'll clean the fish before dinner."

"You mean lay 'em in the river and let the mud turtles eat 'em for dinner," corrected Rob.

"Well, bring a kettle full of water from the spring, and put 'em in that," suggested Stephanie.

"I might just as well clean 'em now as later," said

Rob. "And that's what I'm a-goin' to do. And after that I'm goin' fishin' some more. You can't always be a-tellin' me I got to do this and I got to do that and I got to do the other thing. You're not my boss."

Down toward the spring he traipsed, knife in hand for cleaning the fish, looking mighty pleased with himself.

Stephanie stared after him out of wide open eyes. Why, this was mutiny! Strip, stark mutiny! The kind of mutiny General Washington was always having to quile down. What could she do, she wondered. What could a body expect her to do? The corn wasn't hers any more than it was Rob's. And was it her business, or wasn't it, if Rob wanted to skip the corn and hide out along the river with a fishing pole and let somebody else grub out the tough-rooted sprouts?

"Willie, honey," she called, "you go along now and hunt the shelly bark for Mammy. There's some around this stump right out here in the corn."

Willie came obediently and began to gather long ragged pieces of bark in his arms, while Stephanie chopped the corn rows as clean as a swept floor.

It was almost dinner time when, nearing the end of a row, Stephanie caught sight of a short shadow lying across the corn aisle. Her panicky eyes rested first on a pair of buckled shoes. Up traveled her gaze, slowly, past a pair of knee-length breeches, past a green waistcoat, past a flowing neckerchief, past a swarthy chin to the pock-marked face and the gimlet eyes of Adam Frohawk.

"I see you've improved every shining hour!" rasped Frohawk, indicating with his mocking eyes the finished cabin, the tall corn, the hominy block, and the ash hopper.

The sight of him riled Stephanie to the quick.

"What do you want?" she snapped at him.

"I think—I want my dinner," he told her, as easy-going as if he'd said it was a sunshiny day. "And while you're cooking that, I think I'll have a look around."

He started toward the cabin.

"Don't you go in there!" she ordered him.

Willie was at her heels, his tongue tied with fright.

"What's to stop me?" Frohawk asked. "Not your pappy. He's been gone from the country too long to expect him back."

Stephanie's legs felt like spindly little whips under her. How did Frohawk know where her pappy had gone? And suppose Jonathan didn't come back? Was the land to be Bedinger's just because of that? Hadn't her mammy a right to the land? Hadn't she and Noel a right to it? And Rob and Willie and Cassie? They had all bent their backs clearing it.

Into the cabin strode Frohawk, peering into every corner, staring at the big fireplace, examining every tool and utensil. Stephanie stood in the door watching him.

Rob would be off down the river at a time like this, she complained bitterly to herself.

"I'll get your dinner," she told Frohawk suddenly. "Willie, you run down into the woods and bring me some chips for kindlin'."

"That's a good girl," said Frohawk. "Where's your mammy?"

Stephanie turned away without answering, and left Frohawk in the cabin. Following Willie into the woods, she grabbed him by the shoulders, and looked straight into his eyes.

"We've got to find Rob, Willie!" she said. "Quick. You go down the river that way and I'll go this. And if you find him, tell him to come a-runnin' for his life."

"What if I don't find him?" asked Willie.

"Come back without him, then," she said. "Don't waste any time. And don't go a far piece."

They separated, Stephanie going down the river, Willie going up. In ten minutes they met again.

"Didn't you find him any place, Willie?" Stephanie asked, her voice taut with anxiety.

"No, not any place at all," said Willie. "He said when he left he was goin' so far away he couldn't hear you call him. And he took that Bird Head pistol with him, too."

A wave of anger swept over Stephanie. Tears of helplessness stung her eyes.

"Listen, Willie," she said, "you run lickety-cut to Lonesome Tilly's and tell him to come here as fast as he can."

"Lonesome Tilly?" Willie gulped hard. "Me go after Lonesome Tilly?"

"Yes, you," Stephanie told him, her hand on his shoulder. "Run for your life, and tell him to come here."

Willie stared at her out of eyes that didn't believe she could mean what she said.

"But I—I don't know the way," he stammered.

"Of course you know the way," she told him. "You have to know. A big boy like you couldn't forget so soon."

She gave him a push and set him going, but he turned and faced her.

"I'm—I'm afraid, Steffy!" he wailed. "Make Rob go."

"But we don't know where Rob is," Stephanie reminded him desperately. "Listen, Willie, you've got to go!"

The thought only terrified him the more. He began to cry so loudly that the clearing, Stephanie knew, must be filled with the sound.

"Sh-h-h!" she warned him, laying a finger over his mouth. She stooped down and wiped the tears from his eyes.

"Willie," she said, "recollect you're a patriot, like Noel?"

"Um-hum," he whimpered.

"D'you reckon everything Colonel Clark tells Noel to do is easy? Don't you s'pose lots of things Noel's sent to do are hard, and scary, and make him want to run away? But he never runs away. Noel never, never runs away when Colonel Clark sends him to do somethin' dangerous."

Willie stopped wailing, but he puckered his mouth as he listened to Stephanie.

"Now, you're a soldier, too, and I'm your colonel, and I'm a-sendin' you expressin' to Lonesome Tilly with a message. It ain't a hard job, Willie. He won't hurt you. He likes you, else he'd never have brung you a coon."

"What'll I say to him?" Willie asked in a small voice.

"Just tell him to come quick. And you come back quick, too."

"But what if he doesn't know what I say?"

"Tell him anyway," Stephanie said. "Just try to make him understand, Willie. That's all I ask you to do. Try to make him understand. You might take hold of his hand and lead him a little way. Then come runnin' back like a streak of lightnin'."

Reluctantly Willie turned and vanished into the woods. Now, realized Stephanie, she would have to face Frohawk by her lonesome. She didn't know what she intended doing. Nor did she know what she expected of Lonesome Tilly, if, indeed, he followed Willie home.

She would cook Frohawk's dinner in the clearing, she decided. She would kindle a fire near the east edge of the clearing where she could look now and then at the Tree of Freedom, if she needed to remember what it had to say to her. That was as far ahead as she could plan.

Frohawk was sitting on the hominy block as she came out of the woods. He stared at her as she carried coals of fire from the fireplace and kindled the fire.

"I hear your brother's joined up with Colonel Clark," he said. "The red-hot liberty brother, I mean."

Stephanie's body stiffened with anger. Her blue eyes burned with fury as she met the crafty eyes of Frohawk.

"Another word about my brother, and I—I—"

Frohawk burst out laughing.

Stephanie had meant to tell him she would not cook his dinner, but good sense told her not to invite more trouble than had already made itself at home in the clearing.

Silently she went about frying the fish Rob had left in the spring house, feeling grateful to him now for having cleaned them and left them there. Meanwhile, Frohawk prodded her with questions. Didn't her brother know the war was as good as over? Which way would her mammy be coming home? Wasn't it too bad her pappy never got home with all that hard money Colonel Bowman promised him so he could buy up more land when the court awarded the whole of the Salt River bottom to Bedinger?

It seemed to Stephanie time had never dragged so slowly as that half hour spent in frying the fish and watching from the corner of her eye for Willie and Lonesome Tilly. Wasn't Tilly coming, she wondered. And was it a foolish thing to have sent Willie for him? Suppose something happened to Willie?

At last, out of the north wall of woods, came Willie, half running, looking back over his shoulder as if he thought something might grab him from behind. He opened his mouth to speak, but Stephanie motioned him to silence.

In a minute, the bushes parted and through the leaves Lonesome Tilly thrust his head covered with its tangle of white hair.

Stephanie quailed. Maybe he would be only a hindrance, she told herself. Maybe she could never make him understand what she wanted, if, indeed, she herself knew what she wanted.

She glanced at Lonesome Tilly again as he caught sight of Frohawk. In that instant his eyes burned with curiosity, and horror bubbled up in them like water bubbling in a spring. Without a sound he pulled the bushes together and disappeared.

Stephanie was about to leave her dinner and go to look for him when he peered through the underbrush again, this time nearer to her. Stealthily he inched across the clearing until he reached her. Then he slumped down on the ground at her feet as if he expected her to fend off the critter sitting on the hominy block.

"Well!" said Frohawk. "Looks like we have a visitor!"

Lonesome Tilly blinked his eyes at Frohawk.

"And what a visitor!" Frohawk burst out laughing.

"You stay around, Tilly, till I get dinner ready," said Stephanie, "and I'll give you some."

Lonesome Tilly made no sign that he heard what Stephanie said. He put his hand deep in his ragged shirt bosom. Stephanie watched him fearfully. Did he have it in his little wad of wits, she wondered, to know why she had sent for him?

Frohawk's amused eyes were on Tilly as the old man drew his hand slowly out of his shirt bosom. The amusement changed to horror, however, when he saw Tilly dragging out of his rags a great reddish copperhead.

About Tilly's outstretched arm coiled the snake, its coppery head up, its tongue darting out toward Frohawk.

Frohawk's eyes turned hard as flint. He reached his hand in his waistcoat pocket, whipped out his pistol, and aimed it at the snake.

Like a painter, Stephanie pounced on him, grabbing his arm. The pistol discharged, but the bullet passed below the outstretched hand of Lonesome Tilly and the upraised coppery head of the snake.

Fumbling in his anger, Frohawk began reloading, when, suddenly, up the path from the river came Rob, running straight toward Frohawk, in his hand the Bird Head pistol Jason Pigot had given him.

"Don't shoot, Rob!" screamed Stephanie.

At the sound of her voice, Frohawk wheeled around and looked into the muzzle of Rob's pistol, and over it into Rob's eyes. Slowly he let go of his own weapon, and his hands went up over his head.

"Turn around, Frohawk," ordered Rob. "I'm in charge of things here. Keep your hands up. And start walkin'."

Stephanie stared at them, hardly believing her eyes. It was plain to see Frohawk could hardly believe his eyes, either. Grudgingly he started through the woods, Rob behind him with the pistol pointed at the middle of his back.

"Where're you goin', Rob?" Stephanie asked.

"To Harrod's Fort," Rob told her. "Where else do you think we'd go?"

Stephanie caught Willie by the hand and started after them. "You stay here till we get back, Tilly," she called. "When we get back I'll cook you the best dinner you ever ate."

"What're we goin' to do at the Fort?" asked Willie, hurrying to keep up with Stephanie.

"We aim to ask somebody, Colonel Bowman, maybe, to see that this scoundrel minds his own business till Pappy gets home," Rob answered. "A body don't have to wait till December to tend to that."

15. Neighbors

HERE WAS a thing a body couldn't believe, Stephanie said to herself, over and over, even though she saw it happening with her own eyes. This thing of three young uns, one of them with a Bird Head pistol, marching a grown man into the Fort to turn him over to Colonel Bowman, or to the surveyor, or to anybody with the proper say-so, was like little shavers whooping and hollering around in the clearing, and actually catching a red man when they were only playing like they were catching one.

To Rob, however, the business to which they had set themselves wasn't young uns' play, Stephanie could see. He wasn't taking any foolishness or sass from anybody.

"H'ist it back!" he snapped, when one of Frohawk's arms drooped at the elbow.

"Listen, sonny. Did you ever try holding your hands above your head like this?" asked Frohawk. "A body gets mighty tired after the first hour or so."

"You ought 'a' had that figured out before you got into so much meanness," Rob told him.

If it was hard for Stephanie to believe her eyes, it was harder still to believe her ears. Every word Frohawk uttered, Rob had a ready answer for him, with the Bird Head pistol at the end of it, like the periods in *Pilgrim's Progress* which said you had to stop a minute there and think. If Frohawk struck off in the wrong direction to throw them off the road to the Fort, Rob ordered him back, like her pappy turning Job around with a gee line. If Frohawk claimed he was tired, and wondered if they hadn't all better sit down and rest a spell, Rob reminded him he'd have a long time to rest at the Fort.

Why, here, thought Stephanie, was a job as much to Rob's liking as honey was to bears. Some day, she reckoned, he was going to be a sheriff, or a justice of the peace in Kentucky County, provided, of course, he could go fishing as often as he liked, and hunting, and traipsing around through dark green woods like her pappy. It was a pity, she thought, that Rob had grown clear away from his butterflies. But what a young un was going to be was a thing born in him, she reckoned, and he looked for it until he came to it, and apt as not, it wasn't always what his kinfolks had laid out for him. Uncle Lucien had thought maybe Rob would be a great one to hunt out birds and butterflies and blossoms in the woods, and mount them, and give them names. But Rob, she reckoned, being like her pappy, wasn't turned that way. He liked his butterflies better in the woods and in the fields than pinned to a slab of bark and hung on a wall. But Rob would never see ginger-colored wings striped and bordered with soft apple green hovering over a tall pink spire of the steeplebush, or dull brown cocoons clinging to dull gray twigs of trees in winter, without hearing Uncle Lucien saying wise things in his ear, she reckoned.

On the bank of the branch Frohawk stopped suddenly.

"Keep a-shufflin'," ordered Rob.

"Wait a minute, sonny," begged Frohawk. "I heard something."

They listened, but heard no sound out of the ordinary.

"It was just me you heard, I reckon," said Rob. "And I don't aim to hurt you if you behave yourself."

Frohawk picked up his feet slowly, and put them down cautiously.

"Don't try any tricks," Rob warned him.

Hardly had he got the words out of his mouth when a voice, like an answer, came through the woods—a woman's voice, as clear and as sweet as a church bell ringing out across the wilderness. Stephanie turned cold, not with the fear she might have felt had it been a man's voice, but with sheer gladness that welled up in her now that through the woods was coming her own kind and her mammy's kind.

"We'd better step off to one side, hadn't we, Rob?" she suggested, shivering with joy. No more telling Rob to do this and to do that, she decided. Forevermore a body was to say to Rob, "Wonder if," and "Hadn't we better?" and "If it's all right with you."

The woman's voice had now swelled into a chorus that grew louder as it came closer. Men's voices rumbled and little young un's voices that made a body tingle all over the way he tingled when he heard the first red bird courting in the springtime piped up sweet and clear.

Standing well off the path, they could glimpse the people through the trees now. There were horses loaded with packs. There were half a dozen men swinging along, every one with a long rifle on his shoulder. There were women carrying young uns in their arms, and young uns carrying black kettles in their hands or bundles wrapped in old quilts on their backs.

At the head of the line marched a tall man with gray hair matted on his forehead and stubbly grayish beard covering his chin. There was something about his face and about his long, even stride through the woods that was as familiar as homespun.

Stephanie, with a lump in her throat, gripped Willie's hand.

Suddenly Willie broke away from her.

"Pappy!" he shouted.

Jonathan Venable started, and peered ahead into four pairs of eyes.

"Look out for Frohawk, Rob!" warned Stephanie, though there was no more need to tell Rob what to do than there was to tell General Washington what to do, she reckoned.

"Howdy, Pappy!" smiled Stephanie.

Jonathan stared dumbfounded. "What on earth are you young uns up to?" he demanded. "An' if it ain't that meddler, Frohawk!"

"He was botherin' again," Stephanie told Jonathan.

"He's on his way to jail," said Rob.

"Mister Venable, I—"

Jonathan wasted no words shutting up Frohawk. "You can say your say to Colonel Bowman," he said.

He turned to the travelers. "I thought I was moughty tired," he explained, "but I reckon I'll be downright pleased to finish this little job my young uns started. You can put your play purty up, Rob. I can tow Frohawk in with a rifle, I reckon. Steffy," he added, "you run home an' tell your mammy Jonathan's back an' brung a lot of company to supper with him. They're aimin' to settle."

Back through the woods in the direction of the clearing they turned, Stephanie's feet as light as seeds of milkweed floating through the air.

"So you're the little missy your pappy sets such store by!" said the man walking back of Willie.

Stephanie did not answer right away, although she tried. The cat had surely got her tongue, she reckoned, for not a word could she pry out. She might have been Lonesome Tilly for all the talking she was doing.

After an awkward minute she found her tongue.

"Where'd you come from?" she asked. "All of you?"

"From hither and yon," said the man. "Virginny and Caroliny. The Waxhaw and Great Peedee and the Yadkin. Your pappy gathered us as he came along, a-singin' the praises of Kentucky County. That's why it took him so long to get home. Seems like, as long as he was so close to the Back Country when he was at Williamsburg, he had to drop down to your old home place to fetch somethin' or other to you. So we joined up with him. And here we are. Whatcoat's my name," he added. "Steve Whatcoat."

Stephanie walked on a minute in silence. It seemed overpoweringly good, this prospect of neighbors come to face life with them in the wilderness. But there were things about it she wondered if they knew.

"Did you get your claims straightened out at the Land Office?" she asked.

"Yep," Whatcoat said. "Bought 'em up in Virginny from a speculator that owns land all through here. Had to pay mighty high for 'em, but it was worth it, I'm a-thinkin', to get a fresh start in a new country. Feller intended settlin' out here hisself, but his wife wouldn't come 'count of the red men. The six of us families, we bought up two thousand acres south of your pappy's claim."

"Then Frohawk'll likely be hangin' around your places, too," she told him. "Till December, at any rate, unless Pappy can clap him in jail for trespassin'."

The man laughed a loud, hearty laugh. "I reckon a little thing like Frohawk won't bother us much," he said. "We can make a law for folks like him."

Stephanie turned to glance at him. He was tall and square-shouldered, and fair-haired like a woman, and he walked free and easy as a deer, but without a deer's skittishness. A body could tell by the crinkles about his eyes and the way his chin was set well back atop his breastbone that he knew for a fact the earth was his and he'd always keep it—he and the little towheaded shaver riding on his shoulder opposite his rifle.

"Picked up some mighty good news at the Fort," he told Stephanie. "Colonel Clark's licked the Indians to a fare-you-well at Chillicothe, and not bein' satisfied, he went on to Piccaway and let 'em have the rest of his powder. Not all the British bribes in the country could tempt 'em to come back now, I reckon."

Stephanie's heart fluttered.

"Is Colonel Clark back yet?" she asked. "And his men?"

"Not the Colonel. But his men are stragglin' in."

Stephanie could scarcely hear what more the man was saying to her. Noel might be home, she told herself, when she got there, but she passed lightly over the fact that he would have come by the path they were then traveling, and for certain nobody had seen him.

Stephanie reckoned she ought to be weighted with metal, like Rob's Bird Head pistol, to keep her from rising up and flying. She felt like the mockingbirds that sang so hard they had to fly up and take a little turn in the air just to rest themselves so they could go on singing again. Steve Whatcoat with his towheaded young un on one shoulder and his rifle on the other was pressing hard at her heels, singing snatches of songs, calling back to his friends to look at this wonder and that. Looked like any minute he might have to take a turn in the air like the mockingbirds, too, thought Stephanie, it was so hard to keep his bigness inside himself.

Stephanie glanced back at him shyly.

"Can you read?" she asked.

"You bet I can!" he told her.

"Would you—do you reckon you could learn me how to read?" she asked.

"You bet I will!" he said. "We'll begin as soon as we get to your clearin' and get a drink of water."

"I already know my ABC's," she told him. "Mammy helped me learn 'em."

"Then you're just a whoop and a holler from knowin' how to read already," he said.

As they neared the clearing, Stephanie got a glimpse of her mammy through the trees, standing in the doorway with Cassie beside her, trying to see through the thick green woods. Prissie Pigot's baby had been born all right, Stephanie calculated, and Bertha had hurried home, but she couldn't find hair nor hide of a single young un she'd left there. Some day, soon, thought Stephanie, they would chop down all the trees, and hack a road right past their cabin so that a body could see plainly who was coming and going.

"Steffy!" said Bertha weakly. "Where you been? I called and called."

Before Stephanie could answer, Steve Whatcoat, followed by all the men and women and young uns, all the creel-laden horses, the cattle, and the sheep, crowded into the clearing.

" 'Pon my word and honor!" muttered Bertha. She stared at them a full minute. Then hot, salty tears broke out and ran down her brown cheeks and into the hollows made by her cheekbones.

"Pappy's home, Mammy," Stephanie told her gently, hurrying to her.

Bertha's tears turned into a fresh then, and the miserable memory of long days and longer dark nights of waiting swelled it, and nothing, not even hot, burning shame at crying with so many folks looking on, could stop it till it had run its course.

"Pappy's home, Mammy," Stephanie said to her again. "He'll be here any minute. He had to go back to the Fort for somethin'. And these, Mammy," she added, pointing to the people crowding into the clearing, "these are our new neighbors."

Bertha wiped her eyes on her apron and smiled at the neighbors. "Come right in and sit down and rest yourselves," she said, with the sound of crying still in her voice, "while Steffy and I hustle about and get supper on."

Toward sundown Jonathan came hurrying out of the woods as if his feet itched harder to get home than they had ever itched to leave it.

"Howdy, Berthy," he said, his begrimed, bearded face lighted up with smiles like a shelly bark light in a daubed, dark cabin. "How'd you like the present I brung you? All these new neighbors?"

"You couldn't have brought a finer," Bertha told him.

"An' here's another," Jonathan said, taking a little packet from his shirt bosom. "Turnip seeds. If we plant 'em now, in time to get the fall rains, we'll be a scrapin' juicy sweet turnips all fall. An' here's another."

This time he took from among the plunder heaped around the doorway a deerskin bag rounded from its contents.

"Salt," he said. "Enough to do all winter."

Jonathan looked about him.

"Steffy, where're you?" he called. "I brung you a present, too. If I can find hit."

Again he looked among the willow withe creels, the bulging saddlebags, the black kettles crammed with odds and ends, and the bundles of bedclothes tied with tow string.

"Even looked up one of your old quilts, Berthy, an' brung that along," he said, lifting a quilt-wrapped bundle from the plunder and fumbling with the knot into which its corners were tied.

"Reckon I'm mighty glad I went to the trouble to get this for you, Steffy," he went on, "seein' as how you earned hit for chasin' Frohawk off. You an' Rob."

Bertha stared at them.

"Frohawk?" she asked. "What do you mean, Frohawk?"

Before Jonathan would untie the knot, Stephanie, Rob, and Willie had to get out in the clearing and behave just as they did when Frohawk came snooping in and Lonesome Tilly put a good healthy fear in him with his copperhead.

"Frohawk's bullet went right across here," Stephanie told them, leading the way in the direction which the bullet had taken.

Suddenly she stopped, her face white, her blue eyes full of fire. Stooping down, she lifted the whip of the

Tree of Freedom. Frohawk's bullet had shot through it, leaving it dangling by a thread of the tender young bark, the scarred butt sticking out of the ground like any common sprout to be grubbed out with the grubbing hoe.

"Look what he's gone and done to my Tree of Freedom!" she stormed. "If I could lay hands on him again—"

"What sort of tree?" asked Steve Whatcoat, bending over her to look.

Stephanie explained, trying to cover up her outburst. It was just an apple tree she had planted, she said. A sort of special one. One she had set great store by.

"Well, never mind a little prunin' like that," Steve Whatcoat consoled her. "Come another spring and your tree'll grow again. Give us a good long fall, and chances are it'll be a-growin' new twigs and leaf buds before winter. You can't hardly kill a tree that's got good roots in the ground. And from the looks of this apple sprout, somebody's given it uncommon good care."

Everything was all right then, Stephanie told herself. A body couldn't kill freedom any more than he could kill a tree if it had good, strong roots growing, she reckoned. No matter what passed over the land and possessed the people, you couldn't kill freedom if somebody gave it uncommon good care.

"Whar'd Lonesome Tilly go?" asked Jonathan.

"Apt as not, he skedaddled back home," said Willie.

"Then you skedaddle after him," said Jonathan. "Tell him we're havin' a little gatherin' at our house tonight. Tell him we got salt, an' our new neighbors have brung enough corn meal to last the winter an' to feed all of us on journey cakes tonight. An' tell him he's our special invited guest—him, but not his copperhead," he added. "One of these days soon, Willie, we'll hack out a trail to Lonesome Tilly's cabin. Then you can ride Job when you go expressin' to Tilly's."

A puzzled look clouded Jonathan's face. "Whar was Noel while all this was goin' on?" he asked. "Whar's Noel now?"

"Noel's with Colonel Clark, Pappy," Stephanie said, looking at him steadily.

"What!" thundered Jonathan. "You mean to tell me that boy run off after I told him p'int-blank to stay home?"

"Noel didn't run off, Pappy," said Stephanie. "He went because Colonel Clark had to have him. He was doin' what you told him to do."

"What d'you mean, doin' what I told him to do?" barked Jonathan.

"Don't you recollect you told him what to do in case Frohawk came meddlin'?" asked Stephanie. "You told Noel to take care of him. Well, way we figured it, Frohawk, and King George, and six hundred red men and British generals draggin' a cannon through Kentucky County and scalpin' right and left are all the same thing. The British and the red men showed up first, so Noel went to help Colonel Clark chase 'em."

Jonathan stared at her. "Sounds jist for the world like Noel," he said.

"Noel was doin' his duty the way he saw it," said Bertha.

"But somebody's been makin' out here," Jonathan said, looking about him at the chinked walls of the cabin, at the clean rows of corn, at the newly girdled trees. "As good as any man."

"That was Steffy," spoke up Rob. "And am I glad you've come home, Pappy! There ain't nothin' Steffy won't tackle, and then she tries to make everybody pitch in and help. And it ain't no use tellin' her when she's licked. She just can't understand."

Jonathan looked down at Stephanie, proud and gentle at the same time.

"I reckon hit was wuth all the trouble I took, goin' out of my way to collect that purty for you," he said.

Turning back to the plunder, he unrolled the bed quilt and took from it the gold-and-walnut-framed looking glass that had belonged to Marguerite de Monchard when she was Stephanie's age.

"Thought hit mought spruce up the wilderness a mite," he explained, putting it into her outstretched hands.

16. Home Is the Soldier

STEVE WHATCOAT was so anxious to set foot on his new land that he beat the birds up the next morning, and roused everybody else as he stirred about the clearing, unhobbling horses and loading them. After breakfast, when the settlers cut out through the newly girdled woods to the south in the direction of their land, the Venables went with them. Besides his rifle, Jonathan carried his ax and the maul, Rob carried the frow, Bertha took along coals of fire in a covered kettle, and Stephanie took the preacher feller's copy of *Pilgrim's*

Progress so that Steve Whatcoat could help her with her reading if ever he took a minute from his chopping to sit down and wipe the sweat off his face and rest.

There were six cabins to build. Before the menfolks could begin, however, they had to scatter out in the woods and find game for their dinner. Shouldering their rifles, they disappeared, leaving the womenfolks speculating on the likeliest place to build the first cabin.

Stephanie sat down on the root of a tree and opened her book, but she found it hard to listen to the womenfolks and, at the same time, to make good sense of the words,

> As I walked through the wilderness of this world, I lighted on a certain place, where was a Denn; and I laid me down in that place to sleep: And as I slept I dreamed a Dream. I dreamed, and behold I saw a Man cloathed with Raggs. . . .

Looked like a hill was a mighty pretty place to raise a cabin, said one woman. Then a body could see far and wide. And the dog trot would always be a cool place to sit and churn, or to string beans on a summer morning, or to lean back against the wall and rest in the shade after dinner.

But if she built on a hilltop, another woman told her, she'd spend her whole enduring life lugging things up the hill to herself. If she built in a holler, all the world would come down to her. She favored living in a holler, she said. She'd rather rest more and not look so far.

An hour later, the argument was still running as the menfolks came back with their game—three turkeys with long, bronzed, limber necks dangling; a passel of squirrels; and a deer, skinned and cut up in the thicket where it was shot.

The rest of the day the woods rang with the sound of the ax as men chopped down trees and chipped away bark, notched the big logs, and split the shakes for the cabin roof.

While the men worked with ax and maul and frow, the womenfolks broiled the turkeys and the thick dark steaks of venison, and made rich stew of the tender squirrels over a fire built from the coals Bertha had brought. And everywhere there was talk, talk, talk—little high-pitched talk of young uns hunting wintergreen in the woods, the quiet, even talk of womenfolks, and the loud shouting of menfolks as they dragged logs to the cabin site and skidded them into place on the walls.

Sometimes Stephanie shut out all the sounds but the sound of talking. It put her in mind of a camp meeting song, with everybody joining in. Or of the psalm from the old Huguenot Bible:

Vous tous, habitans de la terre, jetez des cris de rejouissance a l'Éternel.

When the sun went down, the first cabin was almost finished. Then the Venables got together their implements, Stephanie picked up her book from a bed of moss where she had laid it, and they started home.

"We'll be back in the mornin', bright an' early," promised Jonathan. "Reckon the next cabin'll be 'bout a mile farther on, won't hit?"

"Not quite so far," Steve Whatcoat told him. " 'Bout three quarters of a mile, we figured. We aim to settle pretty thick through here. 'Twouldn't surprise me if some time we're a thrivin' town, like that new settlement at the Falls. Or New Bern. Or even Charleston."

"Don't forget to cover the coals tonight," warned Bertha. "We can carry coals from this fire to the next clearin'."

"Pappy," asked Rob, when they were deep in the woods, "can I go huntin' with your rifle in the mornin' before we begin choppin'?"

"I was jist a-thinkin', Rob," said Jonathan, striding along at the head of his family. "Seein' how you did so much with a toy pistol that wasn't even loaded," he added, "I'm anxious to see what you could do with an honest-to-goodness rifle."

"Rob don't need a gun yet, Jonathan," said Bertha. "There's plenty of time for guns later."

"Tell you what, Rob," said Jonathan, paying no mind to Bertha. "This winter we'll do a lot of trappin', you an' me. We can sell the furs down the Mississippi. Maybe we could make us a flatboat, or pick us up one for a song from settlers comin' down from Fort Pitt to the Falls, an' float hit loaded with furs down the river to New Orleans. Soon's we sell the furs we could buy you a brand-new rifle. How'd you like that, huh? Seein' New Orleans whar ever'body talks in French an' wears their Sunday clothes ever'day, an' pickin' out your own rifle?"

There was nothing, thought Stephanie, nothing in the whole, enduring world that Rob would like better than stalking varmints in the winter woods and setting traps for them along the river banks, than floating down the Big River with his loot of furs loaded on a flatboat, and with sometimes a strange, far-off, beautiful city, and sometimes a rifle, shining in his eyes. There was nothing her pappy would like better, either, she thought. It was the medicine he would give himself when, some winter morning, he saw blue smoke curling up from the neighbors' cabins.

The first bright evening star was burning over the cabin as the Venables filed up the hill from the spring. Stephanie saw it first, and made a wish on it, the way her mammy had taught her in the Back Country.

"Star light, star bright,
The first star I've seen tonight.
I wish I may, I wish I might,
Have the wish I wish tonight."

Hardly had she whispered the brief wish than she saw it had come true. Noel, she saw, was already home, standing in the cabin doorway, waiting for them.

At sight of him, Stephanie felt her heart flouncing around under her dress.

Bertha stopped stock-still. She started to say something, but it was plain to anybody's eyes that she was as weak as a newborn kitten. Looked like the summer in the wilderness had taken more out of Bertha than a body thought for. Come winter when the red men would stay put in spite of all the British bribes to pry them out, Bertha would get a long rest. Then she wouldn't spill over like that for everybody to see.

"You back, Noel?" said Jonathan.

At least, Jonathan could find a tongue in his head to speak to the boy. Apt as not, he had been laying to light into Noel when he saw him, but seemed like he was as glad as anybody else to see the young un standing there whole.

"Howdy!" said Noel, coming out to meet them. "I would have been back sooner," he explained, "but there were things I had to do."

Stephanie couldn't take her eyes off him. This was Noel, all right. The outside of him was the same as ever —the same shock of sun-bleached hair, the same freckled face, the same lanky arms and legs, the same steel gray eyes looking straight through things.

In other ways, however, it wasn't Noel, but a

different boy who had come home. This boy wore no sullen look on his face. Gone was the way he drew up into his shell as if he'd been stepped on every time Jonathan spoke to him.

"I was all for comin' back right away, as soon as we settled with His Majesty and the Indians," Noel said, "but Colonel Clark sent me on an errand."

"Your news can wait, I reckon," said Bertha, "long as you're here with it. I never yet heard tell of a body comin' home from war without bein' hungry. After supper you can tell us what kept you."

It was a feast of the biggest and the best the clearing could yield that Bertha got together for supper. And it was a feast for the eyes, too, Stephanie decided, watching this brother helping his mammy, getting a fire going under her kettle, carrying up water from the spring for her, and digging potatoes and scraping them with his knife, natural-like, as if it wasn't a woman's work.

Stephanie went with him to call up the hogs.

"I was mighty worried sometimes, Steffy, you couldn't make out," he confided to her. "You did yourself mighty proud, as far as I can see."

"Oh, things could 'a' been worse," she said, tossing the words off lightly. It was the queerest thing, she thought, how she couldn't remember the number of times they had sat huddled in the dark cabin afraid of their own breathing, now that Noel was home again with some mystifying bright thing inside him.

"Colonel Clark wanted me to carry a message to Governor Jefferson," said Noel, as they sat about the doorway after supper.

They waited, wishing he would hurry.

"He wanted to tell Governor Jefferson I had a callin' to practice law," explained Noel, "and the Governor would oblige him by seein' that I had a chance to read with a good lawyer at Williamsburg."

If a bolt of lightning had struck the doorway where they were sitting, it didn't seem to Stephanie they could have been stunned more completely. This talk of a buckskin going up to Williamsburg to read law books and make a lawyer out of himself fairly knocked a body's breath out. Noel, however, didn't give them time to enjoy their surprise. He had other news.

"While I was in Williamsburg, Pappy, I went to the Capitol and read that Land Law," he said. "Accordin' to the law, that man Bedinger can't claim enough Kentucky land to raise a flag on. Some feller there looked up the records for me, and found mention some place that a man by the name of Nalley had sort of looked over the grant years ago, about 1765, and let that pass for surveyin'. But the law says expressly the land has to be surveyed by a surveyor authorized by the masters of William and Mary College. I went to the College and looked over the names of every surveyor they've authorized since the College was founded, and this man Nalley, if he enrolled there, must have gone fishin' instead of studyin' how to use his compass."

Oh, Noel was talking big as Governor Jefferson himself, thought Stephanie.

"Have you bought pre-emption rights to other land, Pappy?" asked Noel. "With the money Colonel Bowman paid you?"

"Not yet," said Jonathan. "Soon as we get the new neighbors settled, I aim to go to the Land Office an' pay for a thousand acres. I reckon 'twon't be a loss to have another thousand, even if Frohawk can't take this away from me in court."

Noel pulled a piece of paper out of his shirt bosom and handed it to Jonathan.

"You might register this for me at the same time," he said. "It's a military warrant for four hundred acres on the Green River for servin' with Colonel Clark. It's my pay."

Stephanie couldn't take her eyes off Noel. He had gone away with his head hidden under his wing, and he had come back ruling the roost. But queerer than that was the way Jonathan was letting him rule the roost.

"I reckon you can go to the Land Office with me," said Jonathan. "Can't you? You ain't goin' to Williamsburg to read law right off, are you?"

"No," said Noel. "There's not much use learnin' law till you know whose law it is you aim to practice—the new law of a free America or the old British law. I'm countin' on goin' first back over the mountains and join up with the patriots. I figure they need every soldier they can get. And I want to see what's become of Uncle Lucien."

It wasn't so much what Noel was saying that struck a body dumb, as the way he was saying it, upstanding and bold as if he were his own master. Jonathan wasn't understanding him at all. Apt as not, thought Stephanie, Jonathan never would understand Noel, even if he lived to be nine hundred and sixty-nine years old, like Methuselah. But he was listening humble-like, as if he wished he could understand this boy, as if he knew for a fact that this young un of his was worth anybody's trying to understand.

"Reckon me an' Rob mought go out in the spring before corn plantin' time," Jonathan told him, "an' find wharabouts your claim is."

That would be something else for her pappy to do, thought Stephanie, some day when he saw smoke rising from the new cabins down the river and he felt crowded.

"When we finally get our freedom and can make our own laws, then I aim to practice law here in Kentucky," said Noel. "Maybe at Harrod's Fort. Maybe at the Falls. The settlement there's mushroomin'. Named Louisville for the French Louis."

Had Noel seen all the world, Stephanie wondered. The whole, enduring world?

"I brought you some presents, Steffy," Noel said. "Found 'em at a house where I stopped for the night. When the man saw I took a shine to 'em, he told me I could have 'em if I'd dig potatoes for three days. That's one reason I was late gettin' home. I was diggin' potatoes."

He disappeared in the dark cabin loft and came back carrying two books which he laid in Stephanie's hands.

"This here un's called *Arithmetick, Vulgar and Decimal,*" he said, putting a finger on one, "and the other is *A New Guide to the English Tongue.*"

Now it was high time, thought Stephanie, for her to say her say, to spill the thought that had been growing in her own mind while Noel talked of lawyering.

"I'm goin' to teach school in Kentucky," she announced. "I can already read some of the words in *Pilgrim's Progress.* Now I aim to learn everything in these books this winter. Steve Whatcoat'll help me. And when summer comes I aim to gather up all the young uns—the Pigots, and Willie and Cassie, and all the new young uns down the river, and teach 'em to read and spell and cipher."

Noel laughed softly. It was like a miracle from the Bible, thought Stephanie, hearing Noel laugh as if all the tightness inside him had loosened up, and he wasn't lonesome any more, or hurt, or lost in the way he was taking.

"I heard tell of a Dame's school when I was in Williamsburg," he told her. "Girls live together in a big house and learn readin' and spellin' and cipherin' and talkin' French and embroiderin', and a whole passel of other things besides. Reckon you could spare Steffy this winter, Mammy, to go to school in Williamsburg? And reckon we could build her a schoolhouse to teach the young uns in, Pappy, when I get home from Caroliny?"

"Lonesome Tilly'd help build a schoolhouse, I bet," piped up Willie. "And Steve Whatcoat."

Stephanie didn't trust herself to move. Nor to speak. She was afraid she might shatter the bright magic of the words Noel had spoken. Why, she thought, all this was like Uncle Lucien's puzzle cut out of a scrub pine gall. A body got the first pieces together easily enough, but then he struck a snag. He worked on it and worked on it, and he felt like quitting and putting it away in a corner of the loft because he couldn't finish it. Then, he wasn't sure how, he got another piece to fit, then another. And all at once, the rest of the pieces slipped in easily.

"Want to hear a ballet I learned in Virginny?" asked Noel.

He reached inside the door and picked up the dulcimer

where Stephanie had left it. Laying it across his lap, he plucked the strings gently. Now, thought Stephanie, for sure, Jonathan would rise up and claim this was more liberty than he could allow any young un of his to take. But like another miracle straight from the pages of the Bible, Jonathan sat there and listened.

Strumming the strings, Noel sang soft and lonesome-like.

"What a court hath old England, of folly and sin,
Spite of Chatham and Camden, Barre, Burke, Wilkes and Glynn!
Not content with the game act they tax fish and sea,
And America drench with hot water and tea.
Derry down, down, hey derry down.

There's no knowing where this oppression will stop;
Some say—there's no cure but a capital chop;
And that, I believe's each American's wish
Since you've drenched them with tea and deprived them of fish.
Derry down, down, hey derry down.

Three Generals these mandates have borne 'cross the sea;
To deprive 'em of fish and to make 'em drink tea;
In turn, sure, these freemen will boldly agree,
To give 'em a dance upon Liberty Tree.
Derry down, down, hey derry down."

Stephanie sat staring at her pappy with fascinated eyes. Jonathan was patting his bare foot in time to the strumming.

"Seems like I heard that ballet when I was in Virginny, too," he spoke up when Noel finished. "That or somethin' like hit. I can't recollect exactly which."